A MATTER OF WORK ETHICS?

Taylor didn't trust himself inside Cleo's warm, inviting house, still he stepped over the threshold. Cleo took his coat, and prompted, "Do you mind lighting the fire in the family room for me?"

"Not at all."

Taylor was glad f⸻ ⸻ ⸻ think of Cleo. What he ⸻ ⸻ in a romantic setting. ⸻ ⸻ the couch and Cleo joi⸻

Facing each othe⸻ ⸻ eyes mesmerized him.

Taylor reached out and ran a finger along her jaw. He captured her arm and pulled her close—his lips touching hers. He ran his tongue along the curve of her mouth, taking his time to savor her taste.

He would just kiss her. But feeling her hand on his face enticed him to pull her closer. He entered her mouth, tasted her. He leaned her against the couch, needing the feel of her under him for just a moment. Just a moment, he reasoned.

"I've wanted you for so long."

"I never knew," she whispered.

"It was work. I didn't want to mix the two." He hated lying to her.

"What changed your mind?" she asked.

"You," Taylor whispered. "I couldn't wait any longer. But I'm still working for you."

"It doesn't matter."

It did, and Taylor knew it. He couldn't take her until he told her the truth, and he didn't have the authority to do so yet.

BOOK YOUR PLACE ON OUR WEBSITE AND MAKE THE ARABESQUE ROMANCE CONNECTION!

We've created a customized website just for our very special Arabesque readers, where you can get the inside scoop on everything that's going on with Arabesque romance novels.

When you come online, you'll have the exciting opportunity to:

- View covers of upcoming books
- Read sample chapters
- Learn about our future publishing schedule (listed by publication month *and author*)
- Find out when your favorite authors will be visiting a city near you
- Search for and order backlist books from our online catalog
- Check out author bios and background information
- Send e-mail to your favorite authors
- Meet the Kensington staff online
- Join us in weekly chats with authors, readers and other guests
- Get writing guidelines
- AND MUCH MORE!

Visit our website at
http://www.arabesquebooks.com

THE ESSENCE OF LOVE

Candice Poarch

Pinnacle Books
Kensington Publishing Corp.

http://www.arabesquebooks.com

PINNACLE BOOKS are published by

Kensington Publishing Corp.
850 Third Avenue
New York, NY 10022

First Printing: November, 1998
10 9 8 7 6 5 4 3 2 1

Printed in the United States of America

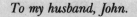

To my husband, John.

ACKNOWLEDGMENTS TO:

Dorothy Prentice for her help on the aromatherapy business;

John Palastro for his help on the duties of a postal inspector;

Tom Hannus and David Bradley for their insights on boating;

As always, Sandy Rangel, my critique partner who has read this novel almost as many times as I have; and my sister, Evangeline Jones, who lost nights of sleep pouring over my horrible handwriting.

Special thanks to all of you.

Chapter 1

Cleopatra Sharp dropped the letter onto the antique-white French desk as if it were a blistering poker sent to singe and destroy her life.

The ink from the twenty-thousand dollar check lying beside it glared at her, its very presence a warning that she shouldn't get too comfortable, because little clues like this were a reminder that the past was always there to strike out when she least suspected it.

Today she merely shrugged at the occasional request for potions or love charms. They barely warranted a blink, but the check she gingerly picked up by the edges was certainly cause for alarm.

Named after the queen she admired for cunning, intelligence and guile, Cleopatra studied in Europe, training in beauty and aromatherapy. Three years ago, she'd started a small mail-order business from an industrial park in Oxen Hill, Maryland, and two years later she'd opened a small store that garnered a loyal clientele. She named it Cleopatra's Aromatherapy after her namesake. Her business was on the cutting edge of a growing, expanding industry.

But clientele would abandon her in a hot minute if they believed for one moment that she'd tricked thousands of dollars from unsuspecting victims.

She pounded a fist on the desk. Cleopatra's Aromatherapy provided a needed and useful product, darn it. More was on the line than her name. It was also the integrity of the ancient therapeutic art she'd studied, practiced, believed in—her very livelihood.

She straightened in her seat, firming her resolve. *Her little company wouldn't come to ruin.*

This resolution didn't keep the chills from creeping through her sturdy frame while she glared at the letter she'd read as she sat in her cozy, minuscule office with its white wicker chairs and floral wallpaper.

From the days of ancient Egypt, oils were used for beauty, healing, and mummification. In ancient Rome, bathers used fragrant oils and ointments to relieve muscle aches, and in present day Japan, odors are used to increase alertness and create positive work settings. In Great Britain where Cleo had studied, hospitals and clinics used aromatherapy to relax patients by decreasing their stress levels and lowering their blood pressure. Cleo knew fragrances have been used to delve into the subconscious and affect behavior.

Only in the last century had the healing powers of these essential oils been lost, only to be replaced exclusively by modern medicine.

Today, however, she knew that the ancient art of aromatherapy had been subjected to scientific tests and, in the last few years, had grown tremendously in respectability and reemerged into modern culture.

Cleo looked up from the paper she held to stare at the diminutive pink flowers, petite green leaf petals, and faint lines of brown stems designed on the wallpaper for its fresh, calming effect. It failed to warm her even a little. An odd, unexpected weariness washed over her.

She scanned the twenty-thousand dollar check that had been mailed to her for her special cancer treatment. The woman's doctor had recommended surgery and chemotherapy.

The woman, however, wanted to try a different route.

Cleo closed her eyes and rubbed her forehead. Not one to dwell in doom, hastily she faced her computer, turned it on and listened to its gyrations as it booted up. Her fingers flew over the keyboard as she typed a letter asking the woman to consult her family and physician before making a decision.

Ending with "Cleopatra's Aromatherapy offers no medical cure for cancer or any other potentially terminal illness," Cleo printed the letter on her blue letterhead.

"Lord, help this woman," Cleo whispered in prayer, hoping the woman wouldn't wait too long to get the treatment she needed.

The day had been productive, with a steady flow of customers. The letter, however, was enough to bring back the nightmare that occurred nine years ago. Long ago, Cleo learned to turn off negative, counterproductive thoughts. The experience nine years ago was in the past, after all. It couldn't touch her here.

With a flourish, she wrote "void" across the check and enclosed it in the envelope with her letter. Placing it in the "to mail" box, she rose to enter her shop, a place that never failed to lift her spirits.

The fresh scent of lavender steaming from the diffuser calmed her nerves.

The muted hammering reverberating from next door brought on feelings of growth and expansion.

"That noise is driving me crazy," Rosebud Collins, her assistant and friend, said as Rosebud floated behind the cash register wearing the long flowing gown she'd chosen as the shop's uniform. Of course, Rosebud was the only person to wear the tent-like garment. The fabric matched the wallpaper. At five-two with flawless ebony skin, Rosebud could get away with wearing almost anything.

This wasn't true for Cleo. Not that she was actively seeking a mate, but the fine male figure next door wouldn't give her a second glance in the shapeless garment. He failed to notice her, even in the flattering suits with short skirts she wore.

Cleo sighed. Every inch of him was hard male personified, from his tensely muscled shoulders and hair-splattered chest, which her fingers just itched to massage.

His cinnamon complexion was a perfect contrast to the short-cropped black hair.

His lean torso she glimpsed—more than glimpsed, to be truthful—when he shucked his shirt as the heat rose to ninety. And those lips—those sinful lips—she just longed to kiss just once.

Um, um, um, Cleo thought and sighed again. Even with her subtle hints, he hadn't spared her a second glance. Best to concentrate on something productive.

"It will only be for a little while longer," Cleo said

and straightened a bottle a browsing customer had misplaced on the shelf.

Rosebud merely rolled her eyes upward and replied with a, "Humph. There's something about that man that doesn't sit well with me."

"Lately, you say that about every man you meet." Cleo perused the cramped shop. She eagerly awaited the day she could open the new space.

"It always rings true, and you know it." Rosebud shook her finger in admonishment. "Mark my words, child. It's never failed me yet."

Cleo declined to answer. Rosebud considered the ringing in her ears a sign that her intuition was correct. And she heard the ringing the moment she met Taylor. Still, Cleo had a cautious respect for Rosebud's intuitions. But she also realized how wide that range tended to be.

Cleo remembered when her mother and Rosebud laughed over their peace and love days in the sixties, they'd talk about Rosebud's predictions.

Whenever one of the women in their group got pregnant, Rosebud would put on her flowing robes and bring out her crystal ball to predict the baby's sex. She was on target fifty percent of the time.

Cleo's dad had called the women a foolish bunch of ex-hippies and walked out when they started their chattering.

Cleo and Rosebud heard more hammering, then curses, as the hammer dropped onto the cement floor.

"I told you you should have hired a reputable company and not some fly-by-night, out of work, handyman," Rosebud snapped, turning toward the door.

"Why spend the extra money? His work is the equal of

a large company. Besides, he had excellent references,"
Cleo murmured as she raced to the next room, hopping
over boards, nails, and buckets.

As a small business owner, she believed in throwing
any business she could to a fellow small business.

Taylor Bradford's string of curses singed her ears as
she neared him. He held his throbbing thumb and
forefinger in his hand.

"Let me see," Cleo demanded, reaching for his hand
when she got to him.

"It'll be okay," he said, biting back more curses
around the women, pain clouding his features.

Cleo grabbed his hand and felt the thumb. It had
reddened, but the skin was unbroken and the bone
didn't seem to be broken. "Can you move it?" she asked

He bent the finger. "Yeah. It'll be okay." He shrugged
off her concern.

"Let's soak it in some eucalyptus and ice water to
help the swelling," Rosebud said.

"I don't have time. I've got to get going." Taylor
began to pick up tools. Such a fuss over a little bang
was ridiculous. But he knew women and their tendency
to baby a man.

"Best get it taken care of," Rosebud insisted. Surprised, Taylor looked at her. He'd sensed antagonism
from her since his arrival.

Giving up the battle, Taylor followed Cleo into the
office and allowed her to push him into the seat behind
her desk. Then she disappeared into the kitchen.

In no time Cleo returned with a bowl of ice cubes
and water. Rosebud put something into the bowl, eucalyptus he guessed from the pungent odor.

Cleo pushed his finger into the mixture.

Even the pungent eucalyptus failed to mask the sweet smell of Cleo. His arm brushed against her breast as she leaned over him. He glanced at her out the corner of his eye. She didn't seem to notice, but Taylor couldn't help it.

Grateful he was sitting at the desk so that only the top of him was visible, he repositioned himself to make certain nothing else was revealed.

As his finger began to rise out of the water, Cleo pushed his hand back in. Taylor stiffened again as his arm brushed her breast a second time. Glancing at her suspiciously, he wondered if it was intentional.

There wasn't a subtle maneuver she hadn't used to get his attention since she'd hired him. Dropping by ten times a day, offering tea or a dessert either she or Rosebud brought in, she'd succeeded, though he suppressed any outward indication of it.

Even now, her angora skirt rode up her thigh every time she bent over, giving him a peekaboo at her long, long legs. Taylor was definitely a leg man, although he appreciated her other attributes as well.

But the matching sweater, though not indecently tight, left his imagination spiraling.

And her smiling creamed-coffee-colored face would entice the most hardened soul with its gentleness.

He couldn't afford to mix work with pleasure. And this was work.

He hardened his resolve, flexed his shoulders, and straightened in his chair.

"You're tense." The sweet balmy voice all but whispered, a rush of cinnamon-apple breath, smelling of the sweet tea, kissing his neck on a sigh. "Loosen up," she whispered again. "Come on. I don't bite. Let it soak for a few more minutes." She patted his hand, straightened, and walked off, leaving her sweet perfume and memories to linger.

She didn't have to bite, Taylor thought as he watched her hips sway. Enveloped in her seductive essence, it took a great deal of self-determination to hold on to his calm. He turned his head and closed his eyes.

Her wiles wouldn't work on him, he decreed. Still, it didn't escape his notice that she was the perfect height for him. With most women, he had pain shooting up his back from bending for a simple kiss. She was tall for a woman. About five-ten he guessed, to his six-four. The top of her head fit just under his chin. What a pleasure it'd be to take her dancing, he mused wistfully.

Concentrate on something else. He closed his eyes and loosened his knotted muscles, opening his tightly shut eyes to focus on the small office. She'd decorated it to get the most out of the compact space without feeling claustrophobic.

"I think I'm feeling better now." He stood abruptly when she reentered carrying a towel.

He reached for it. "Thanks," he said.

Her gentle fingers grasped his hand and examined his thumb and forefinger before he could dry them off.

"Are you sure you're okay? You should soak just a few minutes more."

In a minute he was going to either explode or tumble her on the soft mauve carpet. Why didn't she dress more like Rosebud, a woman who resembled a flower child who should have a flower tucked in her hair walking around a commune in a daze? Rosebud retreated to the store when a tingling bell indicated a customer had entered.

He was saved from further ministrations by a ringing telephone. Cleo gave him a last pat and answered the phone on the second ring.

"Cleopatra's Aromatherapy," came her efficient greeting. "Yes, I do. Let me check my supplies." As she glided out of the office, Taylor wiped off his hand. He tried to flex his finger. The pain was better. *Maybe there is something to this aromatherapy stuff after all.* He shook his head.

Taylor looked at his watch and realized he had twenty minutes to meet Sam Mathers. It would take at least fifteen minutes to get there and park, which meant he wouldn't have time to shower.

He inhaled the flowery scent on him. *I'm really looking forward to being teased in the postal inspector's office. They'll have exaggerated sniffs and remarks about smelling sweet and of fresh flowers,* he thought. It would be too much to expect Sam to ignore it all.

He rolled down the Rodeo's window, hoping the fresh air would drive away some of the scent as he drove in the early rush-hour traffic on the beltway toward Alexandria, Virginia, where he and Sam would meet in a coffee shop.

Early fall was his favorite time of year. The leaves had begun to turn and the Potomac was quieter as boaters docked their boats for the winter. He looked forward to taking his out on a warm weekend. He parked on Alfred Street to walk a couple of blocks to Misha's.

The area was filled with turn-of-the-century town houses-turned-offices and a few quaint shops.

He didn't come here often, but it was a midway point

for Sam, and Misha's had a reputation for good coffee and pastries.

Rush-hour traffic was getting heavier as he walked on Patrick Street. He passed people escaping their offices in a rush to beat the worst of the traffic.

The shop was mostly white with black trim, with little cafe tables and chairs. He selected coffee and apple pie with cheese and ice cream before walking to a table near the window. Sam had yet to arrive. He leaned back and observed the crowd as he sipped on his coffee and slowly ate his pastry treat. It wasn't half bad.

Sam finally arrived wearing a trench coat over a navy suit. Seeing that Taylor was already seated, he went to the counter and put in his order.

"Say it and die," Taylor told Sam as the man neared, making the expected exaggerated sniffing noises as he took a chair across from Taylor. A teasing grin split his face.

"What did she do? Bathe you in flowers?" The man almost choked on a laugh.

Still reeling from the intoxicating memory of Cleo, Taylor gave him a long, hard look, eyeing the plastic dessert menu holder on the round table with an urge to smash it in Sam's face. It was unfair to take his sexual frustration out on Sam.

Even though movies often belabored antagonism among government investigative agencies, he had no problems working with Sam. Sam was down to earth with a sense of humor Taylor could appreciate most of the time. It wasn't Sam's fault Taylor hadn't had sex in a year and now the subject he was investigating was the first woman to tempt his senses in years.

"Tell me what you've got," Taylor said in lieu of an answer.

"Grouchy today, aren't you?" Sam asked. He scratched the sparse spot where his blond hair had started to recede. His hair was combed straight back, curbing his instinct to try to hide the spot. "What'd she do to get on your bad side?"

"Just impatient to get on with other cases," Taylor countered.

They were quiet as the waitress brought over Sam's order. As soon as she left, he pulled out a pad.

"We got a few more complaints. Callers lost anything ranging from 1,000 to 20,000 dollars. We checked the mailboxes they used. A month's worth of mail was stacked there." He took a bite of cheesecake.

With more than a hundred and fifty different box locations in the Virginia, DC, and Maryland Metro area, they could make their rounds time and again. Typically, the defrauders used a box for a few weeks and before the postal inspectors got a hint of a location, they moved on to another box. The scammers lost a lot of cash that way, but they also eluded capture.

"The signature on the back of the canceled check wasn't Ms. Sharp's."

"That's smart of her, isn't it? I've got a copy of Rosebud's signature." He reached in his pocket and pulled out a slip of paper and handed it over. "I doubt Cleo's in this alone," he said flatly.

"I'm still looking for a way into her house."

"As a chemist, she can set up shop anywhere." Sam took a forkful of cheesecake and closed his eyes in ecstasy.

Taylor glanced around as more of the after-work

crowd entered. Relief spread on their faces that the workday was at an end.

"She lives a pretty quiet life. Just seems to work hard during the day and go home most evenings. Her social life is practically nonexistent." They talked a few more minutes before parting.

Taylor decided to return to the shop. If he hurried, he'd get back over the Woodrow Wilson Bridge before the northbound traffic clogged it.

It had been a long time since he'd gone undercover on anything. The postal service liked to use informants now that undercover work was so dangerous. Cleo had bankrupt many families and they contacted the Postal Office daily. Now evenings, when he should be enjoying his boat, were spent hammering in her shop instead.

She seemed the antithesis of a charlatan. As part of the mentoring program with her church, she'd hired Tina Latham, a senior in high school, to train her in all aspects of small business. Tina and her boyfriend, Ashand Tusconnie, hoped to open a lingerie shop after college. Ashand helped with large mail orders. It would be interesting to see if their relationship lasted that long.

With the steady stream of mail orders, and with clients marching in and out of the shop all day, Taylor thought that she made more than enough to support herself. But he knew that enough for him didn't necessarily equate to enough for someone seeking a more elaborate lifestyle.

Either way, he wanted her caught. He wanted her to pay for the many people she'd hurt in order to attain her riches. The short skirts, the come-hither smiles she sent his way, or the subtle strokes of her long fingers that sent shivers through him would have no bearing on the final outcome.

He wondered how long he was going to be able to evade her indirect advances without triggering suspicion. She'd been subtle enough for him to dodge so far, but that could change any day.

While watching her at her best mesmerizing her customers, she had the tendency to make him forget. A dangerous circumstance for a man in his position.

Cleopatra looked up from stocking the shelves as the door opened to admit one of her most loyal customers. Mrs. Charms wore a fitted black business suit. She stopped by at least once a week during her lunch hour.

"Good afternoon. How are you today?" Cleo suspected the woman liked to get away from her chaotic office to talk and wind down.

"I'm out of lavender oil. And I need something for a gift. It's so tense at the office these days and my secretary just helped me finish a major project." She glanced around the store. "I don't know what I'd do without my oils."

"What does she like?" Cleo asked.

"Something dainty, I think," she said and deliberately paused.

"Well." Cleo pursed her lips in thought. "A scented comfort pillow may work, or bath salts in a silk moiré pouch or tall painted bottle." Cleo pulled a pillow off the shelf for Mrs. Charms to examine.

The woman looked around in thought.

"Does she lean toward a relaxed or tense disposition?" Cleo asked.

"The office is so fast-paced and hectic for everyone," the woman sighed.

"Perhaps a diffuser with a relaxing blend? Or a spa basket? This week we have a preholiday special on them. It includes scented body shampoo, lotion, bath soaps, bath salts, a natural sponge, a nailbrush, and a candle."

Mrs. Charms eyes lit up. "That sounds heavenly. I think I'll take one for myself as well. I can pamper myself on the cruise."

She selected the scents.

"May I wrap this for you? There's no extra charge."

"Please. She's such a wonderful worker. I want her to know how much I appreciate her."

"More secretaries wish they had supervisors like you." Cleo put the baskets on the counter.

"It'll take me about ten minutes for the blend and to wrap the gift. Is that all right?"

"Sure."

"Have a seat and relax with a cup of Rosebud's tea while you wait."

Taylor returned at that moment. Cleo smiled at him and he returned that half shy smile she was accustomed to. Cleo wondered if he evaded her because of their working relationship.

"It won't put me to sleep, will it?" the woman asked as she walked smartly toward the table covered with a burgundy tablecloth. A dainty teapot, cups, saucers, and condiments were set out on a tray.

Pride spread through Cleo. It had been the dream of a lifetime to own her own little aromatherapy shop and present her customers with a congenial, welcoming atmosphere to do their shopping. And, she realized, the more comfortable a customer felt in her shop, the more they made excuses to return and spend money.

"It's apple-cinnamon tea today." Rosebud chose the tea of the day for the customers' convenience.

"Umm, it's delicious." Mrs. Charms walked around the store taking delicate sips from her cup.

The hammering started again and Cleo hoped the banging in the background didn't annoy her customer.

"Are you all ready for your cruise?" she asked Mrs. Charms.

"Oh, yes. Henry and I can't wait. In two weeks we set sail. I look forward to that every year now."

Cleo flipped through her file for the exact blend she used for the woman.

Mrs. Charms turned fifty this year, but didn't look a day over forty-five. Cleo had fixed a whole slew of concoctions for the woman. But her ageless appeal was more heredity and the fact that the woman took very good care of herself. It's true that the blends Cleo recommended for her cut down on the blemishes she used to have. But having a healthy lifestyle with a husband of twenty-five years helped immensely.

Cleo only wished she had her own healthy sexual lifestyle to boast about. It had been longer than she wanted to think about since her last boyfriend. Being tall intimidated most men. Taylor was the perfect height, the perfect build, and there was something so trusting and comforting about him that pulled her like a magnet. God was he ever magnetic!

And he looked in the opposite direction every time she tried to get his attention. Sometimes, she even got the feeling that he disliked her somehow. Yet, why? Cleo shrugged her shoulders. She was making a mountain out of a molehill again. They worked well together.

Perhaps what she needed was to be more assertive. Women came right out and asked for what they wanted now. They didn't wait to be asked. In the nineties, a woman couldn't afford to wait patiently for a man to come calling. She had to do the calling herself sometimes.

Cleo knew she wouldn't be that brazen.

Mrs. Charms finally took a seat in one of the delicate eggshell wicker chairs while she waited.

"You must love working here," she said looking around. "It's so pleasant, I could relax all day."

"I do. I wouldn't want to be any other place." Cleo wrapped it with the delicate, feminine wrapping paper the shop used and tied a bow at the top. The entire process only took a few minutes.

"Here you are."

Mrs. Charms placed her cup and saucer on the tray and came over. Cleo rang up the sale.

She didn't get a chance to do anymore of the mail order as the lunch crowd started.

In ten minutes, Rosebud arrived. "You're getting more and more business during lunch."

"True. Word of mouth really spreads quickly."

They worked nonstop. It was two that afternoon before the shop quieted. "I'm going to the office to finish the mail. I've left some orders on the counter. See if you can fill some of them."

There was another bundle of mail Rosebud had picked up on her way in on her desk. Business was really getting better. She opened the letters and separated things into their perspective piles. She let out a sigh of relief when she didn't receive another letter pleading for some special cure.

When Taylor stopped working and came into the store, Rosebud pounced on him.

"Oh, you're just in time," she said. "I need you to bring a few boxes out here. We got new supplies and they need to be keyed in and stocked. If we do it together, it'll go much faster."

"I can do that with you later, Rosebud." Cleo said, entering the store.

"But we're out of some of this stuff. We need it on the shelves. We're going to get a new rush in another hour." She looked puzzled at Cleo. "He said he'd be willing to help out in the store after hours."

"You're right. I don't know what I'm thinking."

"You've been out of it all afternoon. Is anything wrong?"

"Of course not. Business couldn't be better."

The entrance of a customer ended the conversation. Taylor retrieved the boxes from the storage room and he and Rosebud worked together until the rush.

Every chance he got, he took a surreptitious peek at Cleo. He noticed an unusual edginess in her. Her forehead was often drawn, in contrast to the easygoing, relaxed expression she usually wore.

He knew something was definitely wrong when she didn't give him those sweet smiles or brush past him a time or two to get his attention. Perhaps he should change tactics. If he were more approachable, she might confide in him. Now, with his standoffish attitude, he was the last person she'd unburden herself to.

The trick was to be a friend and not have to fight to

stay out of her bed. Not that, under different circumstances, he wouldn't love to be there.

The next time she looked his way, he smiled at her. She did a double take but didn't smile back.

What now? he thought.

Chapter 2

"Don't tell me you bought another piece of furniture." Rosebud put her hands on her small hips and watched Taylor and Ashand grunt under the weight of the nineteenth-century table as they carted it into the store. She squeezed around it, inspecting it from every angle. Suddenly she smiled in exasperation as one would do with a child. "What happened to your restful afternoon off, Cleo? You haven't had one in three weeks." She shook her head at her godchild.

"I got the house cleaned this morning, leaving the entire afternoon with nothing to do, so I went to a garage sale." When the men set the heavy piece down, Cleo stroked a hand lovingly over the scarred painted surface anyone else would call ugly. She saw possibilities.

"I just couldn't resist it." She looked up at Rosebud. "Can't you just see it bleached white and stained?" She put a finger to her pursed lips in thought. "I have two of them and I think I'll put them in the center of the new store to display eye-catching gift packages. For the open house we'll put snacks on one and gift boxes on the other." Glancing up, she observed Taylor and

Ashand struggling with the second one and ran to open the door for them.

"You're so creative," Tina said. "Seeing what you've done before, I know this will turn out beautifully." As always, the teenager had a pad and pen in hand, taking notes for when she opened her own store.

Cleo regarded the teenager, remembering being just as hopeful and eager at that age. She'd promised herself after her fiasco in college, if she got the opportunity she'd steer teenagers in the right direction, not gain their trust and betray them.

"Why do you put so much work into your shop? I mean, you barely take any time off," the teenager asked.

"I'll take more personal time after the open house and Christmas rush." She looked at Tina's rapt teenage face. "I love what I do."

"I went shopping for a homecoming gown last week and the salespeople barely helped at all. Now, I understand why people feel special when they come here. We take really good care of them."

"When customers feel special and cared for, they return again and again." The smile left Cleo's face, replaced by sudden seriousness. "People spend hard-earned money here. The least we can do is give them the respect and courteousness they deserve.

"If you give your lingerie customers good, personal attention and constantly reemphasize that to your sales staff, your customers will stay loyal to your business. When they need a pick-me-up, they'll come spend money in your store for it." Cleo smiled.

Cleo had gained everyone's attention. Why couldn't that be enough for her? Taylor wondered. Why delve into the illegal? Why care about customers on the one hand and steal from them the next moment? He couldn't picture her as the hard-hearted woman bilking twenty-thousand dollars each out of desperate senior citizens.

This case frustrated him more than any he'd worked on, not that it was more difficult than most because it wasn't. It was the paradox of Cleo that set his teeth on edge.

Taylor tried to remember that he'd lived long enough to know that surface presentation and looks were a poor judge of character.

Ashand leaned on the wall and Taylor stood nearby crossing his arms as he and the teenager watched the women debate where the tables should go.

Even stretching the imagination, Taylor couldn't picture anything lovely out of the dirty, scratched, and scuffed up furniture.

He'd seen pieces like this stored in attics when he visited some of his older relatives in North Carolina. They never threw anything away.

"You should have rested or visited a museum today. Not work," Rosebud reprimanded. "And this was work. Course I doubt you know the meaning of the word *rest.*" The older woman threw her hands in the air.

"Browsing quaint shops, flea markets, and garage sales is restful," Cleo countered.

The ladies' preoccupation with their conversation gave Taylor an opportunity to talk to Ashand. The teenager stood around six feet and wasn't overly muscular. He stopped by to take Tina home almost every night. This was Taylor's first close-up encounter with him. Usually the boy didn't hang around.

"You guys must work out a lot," Taylor said. Ashand

seemed to ignore the women. Probably accustomed to their fussing and debating every issue.

"Got to stay in shape for football," the teenager said.

"Yeah? What position do you play?" Taylor crossed his arms and rocked on his heals. He looked familiar.

"Quarterback."

A leader, Taylor thought and wasn't surprised. He must have seen his picture in the paper.

"Senior?" Taylor asked.

"Yeah, got a scholarship to Grambling next year." A half-smile tilted his mouth. "Me and my buddy'll be playing together next season. He plays guard."

"Good for you." Taylor meant it and hoped he could get him away before Cleo dragged him into trouble and ruined his future. He didn't have the deep-set eyes, combative behavior, or the swelling that were only some of the exaggerated effects that bespoke of the steroids so many athletes took. "Is Tina going there?"

"No, She's going to Howard. That way she can still work with Cleo."

His gaze flicked to the women as their voices rose, the three of them now squabbling over where the tables should go—in front of the doors or at the checkout counter for impulse spending.

Excitement exuded from Tina at being a part of the expansion and decision-making process. Cleo taught as well as listened, Taylor mused.

Taylor often heard Tina say, "Ashand and I will do this or that when we open our own store after college." Taylor wondered if the relationship would survive college, since many young people fell in love and found partners there.

"Where do you want us to put these?" Taylor asked.

It was closing time and Ashand kept looking at his watch. They had school tomorrow.

"In the storage room. Once we sand this paint off, the wood will show through beautifully." She pulled off a piece of loosened paint. "It looks like oak underneath," Cleo added with one last contemplating glimpse.

Taylor and Ashand hefted the heavy furniture into the cramped storage area with barely enough room to hold the pieces. Stacks of boxes waited for unpacking when the new store opened next week.

"We may as well take a look at your work," Cleo said as they wiped the grime off their hands. She always looked for excuses to visit that area. At least he knew she was pleased with what he'd done. Taylor received a certain satisfaction from that. Cleo was an exacting taskmaster.

She opened the door that separated the areas.

"You do some beautiful work." She ran her delicate long fingers across the wood.

He heard a mumbled, "Should be at the pace he's working," from Rosebud, and chose to ignore it.

Cleo twirled around the room. "I can't wait for this extra space to spread the products out." She continued to peruse the room. "Just look at the fine detail."

She glanced at Taylor. "You're an artist," she said softly and he knew she felt it.

Pride at her appreciation of his work squared his shoulders. Her enthusiasm always carried him along with her. How could it not, with her emotions clearly reflecting in her hazel eyes?

She'd given him carte blanche with creative touches

and he'd added one or two. You'd think he handed her the Brooklyn Bridge the way she carried on.

Taylor cleared his throat. "Thank you. I hoped you'd like it." Not for the first time did he feel like a fraud when she threw those charming innocent-looking eyes his way. And again he thought, how could someone who seemed so honest—who carried her heart on her sleeve—be so deceitful?

"Well, I've got to leave in time to stop by the hardware store."

"Don't forget to save the receipt," Cleo reminded him as he left.

He smiled, remembering the last time he forgot. He had received a lecture on taxes and proof of purchases. It didn't stop her from recording the cost. He waved and left.

Cleo gazed at Taylor's departing form encased in snug jeans. He sure was a lot of man, she thought as they all re-entered the store.

Ashand cleared his throat.

"If you're through with us, Tina and I'll be leaving too."

"Thanks for your help," Cleo said.

After the teenagers left, Cleo and Rosebud went back into the shop for the nightly cleanup and shelf restocking. Another half hour to go before their day would end.

"So tell me about this new boyfriend." Cleo dusted the shelves. They had to dust every night because of the carpentry work next door. "How are things going?"

"So-so. Fine, I guess."

Rosebud opened a box of lemongrass. "I got a letter from Ronald yesterday." Ronald Lawrence was in the

Army. Rosebud had dated him for years. Four months ago he'd relocated to Greece for a two-year stint.

"What did he have to say?" Cleo knew Rosebud was in love with Ronald.

"Keeps telling me to wait for him." Deep in thought, she held a bottle of essential oil.

"Are you?" Cleo watched her lifetime friend carefully.

Rosebud had attended high school with Cleo's mother and they had lived their free-spirited, hippie-like life in the sixties. Later, however, Cleo's mother settled down into a more traditional life, but Rosebud had never made the complete transition.

Some people just didn't fit into the stressful career path that everyone seemed bent on today.

"Why should I wait?" Rosebud sighed. "He doesn't want to get married. I'm ready to settle down. I told him when he left for Greece that six years was long enough to wait for any man," she huffed.

Cleo wouldn't point out to her friend that six years ago, she wasn't ready for marriage, either. "Is Albert ready for marriage?" This rebound relationship with Albert Wilson started a month ago.

"We haven't discussed it. The relationship's too new." Finished with the lemongrass, Rosebud started stocking the eucalyptus. "I don't know enough about him to even consider marriage. And he's not my Ron."

Cleo gave her a sad smile. It looked like the women of Cleopatra's Aromatherapy were destined for unrequited love.

Not that she was in love with Taylor, she corrected.

She merely had trouble explaining the strange sensations she got.

"Anyway, Albert loves this area. He's all settled in now and his mother is something else. She's the feistiest old lady. We met in the lobby one day."

"He's still living with his mom?" Cleo knew how tricky that could be.

"Her social security doesn't cover all her expenses. He kind of helps her out. Anyway, he works nights and I work days. He comes by some mornings before I leave for work and brings me breakfast. Isn't that sweet of him?"

"It is. Sounds like the man of your dreams."

"I don't know. He seems a little too perfect at times." She glanced at Cleo, a bottle of oil hovering in her hand. "Ah, listen to me, just creating problems. I should be grateful he walked into my life at the right time. I had to cook breakfast for Ronald every morning. It's nice to have someone look out for me for a change."

Cleo wondered how long it would be before Rosebud realized what was plain to her. Ronald was a decent man. When the two first met, they were both free spirits. Now that Rosebud was ready for settling down, she hoped Ronald would miss Rosebud enough to compromise. And she hoped Ronald made it back before Rosebud settled for Albert.

Albert wouldn't last. But she couldn't tell Rosebud that for fear that she'd try to prove her wrong. Cleo only wished a certain male felt something for her. Because every time he walked in her store, her heart skipped a beat.

Cleo returned to her work.

"You may want to finish going through your mail before you leave."

"I've sorted it and went through the important ones. I'll take the rest home with me."

Cleo slipped her keys into the cash drawer the next morning. An overturned truck on the beltway had her running later than usual. It was 9:30 and in half an hour the store would open, leaving her little time for morning prep.

She brewed a pot of tea.

Five minutes later, Taylor walked in, wearing his usual uniform of jeans and a T-shirt.

"Morning," he murmured, and immediately went to work, barely looking in her direction.

Such a quiet man, Cleo thought. Often she would initiate conversations with him only to have them cut short as he returned to work. Of course she wouldn't want him loafing on the job, but still, he could be more sociable.

Cleo poured herself a cup of tea and a second one for Taylor. She had time yet before she'd have to open the doors. Awkwardly, she opened the kitchen door.

"I fixed tea for you." She padded over to him, skirting tools and building materials.

He glanced at her but finished working with the electrical switch before standing.

"Thank you," he said pulling off his gloves to wrap his hand around the proffered tea.

Cleo sipped on her own tea while glancing around the room. "You know, I wondered if the shelves should go in the other direction."

Taylor pulled his cap off his head and repositioned it in a frustrated gesture. "We'd have to rework the whole plan."

"If it's best for the store, I wouldn't mind," she added cautiously, not wanting to annoy him.

Every other day, she came in with new ideas. Taylor hoped to get a chance to snoop in the kitchen this morning while she was busy. "If you change directions, the sides of the shelves would face the customers when they entered. The way you've arranged them, they'll observe your products first."

"I was thinking of focal point shelves at the end of the aisle with pretty displays of what's on each row of shelves. Wouldn't that work better?"

Every time she gestured with her hand, the emerald-green dress rose two inches and Taylor's eyes wavered with the hemline.

Her face, all animated and fresh with a minimum of makeup, was not the first thing he wanted to see in the morning. Nor was the red lipstick she wore that he itched to kiss off.

"Do you see what I mean?"

Taylor looked at her perplexed. He'd missed the last few words but he nodded anyway and said, "Yes, I do." He cleared his throat. "If that's what you want . . ."

"Well, I'm not sure. You're the carpenter. What do you think?"

"Anybody in there?" They heard Henry Clark, her bookkeeper/accountant call out.

"In here," Cleo responded.

At sixty and a retired civil-service worker, he visited twice a week to keep up to date on Cleo's bookkeeping. He only maintained three accounts. Just enough to keep busy, but not enough to interfere with the vacations he liked to take with his wife.

They had been visiting his son and daughter-in-law for the last two weeks and had toured Disney World.

"Have you met Taylor Bradford?"

"No, I haven't. How are you, young man?" Henry approached Taylor.

"Good, thank you." Taylor extended a hand. The older man's grasp was firm and quick.

"Henry is just back from his trip to Florida," Cleo explained. "How was it?" she asked him.

"Glad to be back. About wore me out." He wore sweats because he went for a jog after leaving her shop.

"But you and Katherine enjoyed seeing Mickey and Sea World, didn't you?"

"Played a little golf. Katherine enjoyed it. That woman still gives me a good workout in golf," he said affectionately. He glanced at Cleo and turned toward the office. "Came by to pick up your files."

"I kept up the records while you were away. I recorded everything on the computer just as you requested. The receipts are in the accordion file on the desk."

"Good, good. I've got a lot to catch up on. Just going to go through your receipts and print out some files for my records. Don't want it piling up."

"It's all yours." Cleo watched him disappear into her office, then glanced at Taylor. "We'll go with the original plan," she said and didn't miss his expression of relief when she left.

Rosebud had opened the store.

"Must have been a boring vacation if he was itching to get back here," Rosebud muttered in an undertone.

"Will you be quiet?" Cleo whispered, casting quick looks at her office.

"Humph." She returned to packing the shelves. "Oh, I stopped at the post office on my way in. You got lots of letters today."

"Thank you." For the last three years, Cleo viewed mail with excitement, but now she looked at it with trepidation.

When business slowed, Cleo closeted herself in her office and left Rosebud to wait on customers.

Stealthily, Taylor trekked into the kitchen, quietly opening the cabinet where Cleo stored her mixes. All of the bottles were labeled. He took a whiff to make sure the items were actually as they were labeled.

He also opened packages to see if any pills were harbored somewhere. He had snooped halfway through and reached for another bottle when he sensed he wasn't alone. He waited a moment, still holding the bottle when he glanced slowly toward the door. Rosebud was studying him from the doorway. He continued to take the top off a bottle and smelled it as if he belonged there.

"These don't smell anything like I'd think they would," he said to her.

"Most people haven't smelled them in their natural form." She crossed her arms with a frown. "Why are you in here?" she asked.

"I was getting ready to fix myself some coffee and couldn't find the beans."

"They're in the refrigerator."

"Thanks." He pulled open the refrigerator door and

rooted around behind lunch bags and drinks before he grasped the coffee. "I never would have guessed, hidden the way it was." He took the bag to the coffeepot he kept in the room he was repairing.

That was a close call. Rosebud had a suspicious nature. If he wasn't careful, he'd soon be out of a job.

Rosebud watched Taylor's retreat. She found less and less to like about him. He was always snooping around. Immediately, she pounced on Cleo.

"Cleo, I still don't trust that man." Righteous indignation had her pacing back and forth.

"Calm yourself, Rosebud. What did he do now?" Cleo asked, resigned that at least once a day Rosebud found something Taylor did to complain about.

She stopped pacing in front of Cleo's desk long enough to point to the kitchen and say, "I caught him snooping in the cabinets in the kitchen."

"I've got nothing to hide in there. He can look all he wants." Cleo dropped the letter she was reading on the desk, giving Rosebud her undivided attention.

"Said he was looking for coffee beans."

"Did you tell him where they were?"

"Yeah, but if he was looking for coffee, I'll eat my buttons," Rosebud declared.

"Not a nutritious diet, is it?" Cleo brushed the suspicion aside.

"I'm keeping an eye on that man," Rosebud wagged a finger, but the tingling entrance bell prompted her to leave the office.

Cleo was too disturbed to think about a snappy comeback like saying *she* would keep an eye on the good parts. In today's mail, she'd received three more letters requesting her miracle cure.

Cleo rubbed a hand across her forehead. Why was she getting these requests? She'd been in business three years and never received requests like these.

She'd been closing her eyes, hoping the problem would go away. The dilemma wasn't going to just up and disappear. Some action was required. But what?

In one of the letters, the woman stated that she'd lost the ad she'd received in the mail, but when she searched the internet she was fortunate enough to discover Cleopatra's Aromatherapy home page. She was praying that Cleopatra would help her ailing relative.

Cleo dropped the letter and turned on her computer. She got on the Internet and did a search on her home page to make sure something hadn't been placed illegally in her space.

The usual page came up. Just her logo, catalogue of products, prices, and gift baskets. Nothing about special cures for diseases.

Cleo didn't advertise in magazines. Was someone else using her name? Cleo did a general search on Cleopatra's Aromatherapy and waited while the Internet did its search. Several links came up, all of them referring to the link to her page. She was linked to professional organizations, so it was expected that she would find several hits. The Internet only found one page linking to hers.

But wouldn't that seem suspicious? Anyone advertising a cure for that amount would be quickly investigated for fraud by the postal service.

Cleo got up to pace the office. It was three weeks ago when she received her first request. And why wasn't she receiving more mailings? Then Cleo thought of the exorbitant amount and realized few people had that kind of money to spend on miracle cures.

She wished she could go to the authorities. She didn't dare. They'd probably lock her up for false advertising. But how was she to discover who was using her company's name, and why?

The first step would be to write this woman and ask her where she saw her name. At least that would be something.

Cleo quickly typed out the letter on the computer and printed it out on blue letterhead. She asked the woman to call her toll-free number.

A huge weight fell from Cleo's chest now that she had taken some action. Once she discovered where these people were getting her name, she could take steps to have it stopped.

The inactivity had caused her anxiety. But she couldn't wait to find out who did this. She ran an honest business and hated the fact that someone was using her good name to steal from people.

Like it or not, she remembered the college ordeal like it was yesterday.

Chapter 3

It had been an ordeal that still wakened Cleo in nightmares. Cleo had met Mrs. Ryker, the sweetest petite woman who looked to be in her seventies, while she was in college. The woman shopped at the health-food store

Cleo worked in during her junior and senior years. Cleo thought she stopped by twice weekly more for companionship than the products they sold. She'd totter in during a lull in business and stay on to talk awhile. Cleo would give the woman her undivided attention.

Suddenly, she began to age and visited less frequently. In months, Cleo had watched her age ten years. Cleo often asked her if she could help her in some way.

Finally one day, Mrs. Ryker had burst into tears, her frail shoulders shaking. Instantly, Cleo grabbed a box of tissues, rounded the counter, put her arms around the woman's small shoulders and guided her into the storage room, shuffling papers off the chair for her to sit.

The other clerk tended to customers.

"I've spent all the insurance money my husband left me on Judy Gross's famous cure for my brother. I love him so much and I just can't bear him leaving me." Mrs. Ryker held her lips together to still the trembling, but it didn't work. It crushed Cleo's heart to see her in this state.

"What famous cure?" Cleo asked, patting her hand to urge her on.

"Her liver treatment, but it didn't work. He's getting worse by the day," Mrs. Ryker answered. "Nothing's working. The doctor . . ."

"But this is a health-food store, not a druggist," Cleo said in disbelief.

"She said she had a special cure and my neighbor said it worked for him."

"How much did you spend?" Cleo asked wondering if the woman was becoming senile. Maybe Cleo should try to contact a relative to look into her affairs.

"Twenty-five thousand dollars. I know it may not be a lot to some people, but it's all I had left."

She blew into a tissue. "Medicare doesn't pay for all the medicine I need." Cleo handed her another tissue and she wiped her nose with it. "Social security doesn't pay for all my bills. I do a little sewing for people, but that doesn't pay it all either. I'll lose my house. I won't be able to pay my taxes and electric bills."

How could this possibly be true? Cleo had wondered, as the woman continued to unburden herself. Judy was as trustworthy and as fair a boss as they came. She always trusted her sales staff and listened to their advice for improvements for the store. All her workers loved her.

To think that she would delude and steal from senior citizens who could ill-afford it was unthinkable. Cleo pondered her next step.

At least the bank would have copies of the canceled checks. Unless she paid in cash.

"Do you have receipts or canceled checks?" Cleo asked, weariness gnawing in her stomach.

"Yes," she nodded stiffly. "I keep all my papers in the living room drawer."

"Let me take you home and you can show them to me. Will that be all right with you?"

"Okay. Do you think you can get my money back?" the woman asked hopefully.

"I can't promise you that, but we'll see what can be done." Cleo held Mrs. Ryker's elbow as she led the woman to her large old Bonneville with scattered rust spots. She looked like a child perched on the seat.

Mrs. Ryker had stored all the receipts in an envelope. In that envelope were five checks—five-thousand dollars each—made out to Judy Gross. The signature on the back was the unmistakable flourish Cleo recognized so well. She stared blankly for seconds.

Dumbfounded, Cleo could only whisper, "Do you have any of the medication she sold your brother?"

"Yes. I wanted her to check and see if she gave me the right medication." The woman dug into her purse, pulled out the bottle and handed it to Cleo. Opening it, Cleo dropped one of the pills into her hand. It was a vitamin they sold for eight dollars in hundred-pill bottles in the store. Only the bottle and label had been changed.

Oh, my Lord, Cleo thought. Her head was spinning as if she'd entered the twilight zone.

"Mrs. Ryker, I'm going to call the police. May I use your phone."

"What's going on?" she asked, frightened, pulling the tissues to shreds.

Cleo sat beside her and took her frail hand in her own. "This medication isn't worth more than eight dollars," she whispered.

A flush of panic crossed her face. "What!" she said and looked as if she'd faint any minute. She jumped up to pace, then sat again.

"I'm sorry. It's a vitamin. Not medicine or a cure for anything. I have to call the police right away. Will you be all right?"

"Oh, all my money is gone!" Mrs. Ryker clutched her chest with both hands.

"Just hold on, all right. I'll do what I can to help you." Cleo hugged the woman as her frail shoulders shook, fresh tears leaking from her eyes.

Cleo notified the police immediately, hoping Mrs. Ryker could recover some of her money and hold on to her house. Cleo waited with Mrs. Ryker for them to arrive. By this time, the woman was almost comatose. Too afraid to move as the truth slowly sank in.

The officers took a report and Cleo's address and told them someone would be in touch.

The next day had been a nightmare.

Cleo and the salesclerks at the store had been taken in for questioning and interrogated once a day over several week's time.

Later she discovered the postal inspectors had already gathered evidence on Judy Gross. They'd received numerous mail complaints on her employer. That very day they stormed the warehouse where Judy ran her sleazy mail-order business, thousands of boxes of pills scattered about as if everyone left in a hurry.

Judy Gross had escaped and so had the other bosses who were involved in the illegal business. Unfortunately, they were never found.

Cleo and the other salesclerks in Gross's shop hadn't known the mail-order business even existed. The authorities thought Cleo had warned the woman, enabling her and her disreputable group to escape capture.

The store was merely a funnel for the money she made illegally.

Recalling the ordeal, Cleo ran her hands up and down her arms as goose bumps sprang on her arms. Soon her whole body grew cold at the memory.

She was livid that they'd badgered the innocent instead of spending more time searching for Judy Gross. Had they acted quickly, they'd probably have caught her. Instead, they tried to blame Cleo.

Cleo certainly wasn't going to trust them this time

around. She'd do her own research—her own investigation.

As she felt the past reaching out to grab her by its ugly tentacles, she tried to remember that it was nine years ago and it couldn't touch her now.

She ran a clean, honest business. There had to be a reason she was suddenly receiving letters for miracle cures and she didn't dare go to the authorities for help this time. They'd proved to be worse than no help.

Cleo shook her head over her active imagination. Perhaps it was a coincidence. Only she didn't believe in coincidences. Judy Gross wouldn't dare show her face in this area. Too many people knew her.

"Cleo, did you mix the facial solution for Mrs. Brown?" Rosebud asked.

"Yes, I did. It's in the kitchen," Cleo said in low tones. "I'll get it for you."

"All right."

Cleo plucked the label she'd typed off the desk and hurried into the kitchen for the facial solution. Taylor held the bottle under his nose.

"What are you doing?" she asked Taylor, her brows puckered with the suspicion Rosebud had planted. She walked toward him.

Taylor leisurely lowered and recapped the bottle, then set it on the table. He turned toward Cleo as if he had every right to be inspecting the bottle. "What's this for?" he asked, all innocent.

Suspicion cleared, Cleo immediately explained, ready to indoctrinate anyone interested in her art and love.

"This is a facial solution for oily skin. Sometimes

when skin is dry, it secretes more oil to compensate and the drying solutions only makes the skin drier. The astringents defeat the purpose." Cleo reached for the bottle.

"I have to get this to a customer."

Taylor handed her the eight-ounce bottle and she slapped a label on it.

"If you're interested in oils, I have pamphlets and I'll be happy . . ."

"You got that oil yet," Rosebud rushed in looking suspiciously at Taylor.

"Here it is." Cleo handed it to her. "Do you need help out there?"

"No, it's slow."

Cleo opened a cabinet and plucked a bottle off a shelf. Opening the small bottle she passed it back and forth under Taylor's nose as one would sniff perfume.

"Lemongrass," she said. "I dilute it with water for cleaning. It's an antibacterial and deodorizer. For centuries it had been used in India to treat fever. It's also an insect repellent. If you get little bugs in your house the beginning of spring, clean with this."

She let him test about four bottles while telling him the properties, its uses, and how it was used for centuries before he said, "You're very knowledgeable about this, aren't you?"

Taylor leaned against the counter and crossed his arms, drawn into her enthusiasm.

"I should be. I trained in London."

That must have been after graduation, Taylor thought. "Why there?" he asked.

"I could get the best training for beauty and aromatherapy. Europeans have used this for years while it only recently caught on in the States.''

Taylor realized she forgot to make advances toward him while she was deeply involved in her aromatherapy. He wondered if he should be honored or humbled.

He listened as he observed her black slacks paired with a long-sleeve gold blouse that reached just below her hips. Black needlepoint stitching on the collar and sleeves kept it from being plain. On her feet, she wore black flats in lieu of heels today.

They stood side by side, slightly facing each other. Mixed with the other aromas was her perfume that kept teasing him. Her hair, barely tucked under, reached her shoulders. Gold earrings dangled from her delicate lobes. Her eyes danced with animation.

And the skin surrounding the gold necklace that reached just above the V collar pulled his attention. He longed to reach out and follow its lines with his fingertips.

He longed to kiss her just once.

Suddenly, Cleo stopped speaking.

Taylor's gaze flew up to her slightly flushed face, her mouth shaped as though she'd stopped talking in mid-sentence, her eyes radiant.

He felt like an idiot, staring at her. Thirty years old, staring at a gorgeous woman without a sensible thought springing to mind.

''Well,'' he said. ''I think I'll go . . . ah, to McDonald's for lunch.''

Cleo looked at his hand. ''I thought that was lunch.'' She pointed to the bag.

''Oh, yeah.'' He lifted his bag. *Really bright move here, Taylor,* he thought.

"You can eat in the kitchen. I won't mind. I'll join you." She went to the fridge and pulled out her own orange Tupperware pack.

Taylor would look foolish if he left, so with no other recourse, he dropped his bag on the table and pulled out a chair for her.

As he sat facing her, he realized he was drawing closer to Cleo whether he wanted it or not.

"I still say we can't trust that carpenter you hired," Rosebud said as they cleaned the shop that evening.

"Why?" Cleo's hand stilled near the on switch on the vacuum. The progress, albeit little she'd made with him, still felt good. She didn't tell Rosebud she'd caught him sniffing the products. It was an innocent gesture, after all.

It had crossed her mind that perhaps it was Taylor behind this fraud.

Don't be silly, she admonished herself. Just because he's smelling your oils doesn't mean he's involved in fraud. Tina and Ashand had done the same thing when Tina started working there. Cleo warned herself to not put too much into Rosebud's vivid imagination.

"I've told you over and over, I've had a feeling about that man since he got here."

Cleo relaxed again.

"I don't see anything suspicious in him wanting to smell some of the products here. He's just curious. People who've never been in a place like this usually are," Cleo assured her.

"You can trust him if you want. I'm keeping an eye on him." Rosebud shook her head. "You need somebody to look out for you, else people will take advantage of your trusting nature.''

Rosebud barely trusted anyone. Cleo and her mother and Ronald were the few exceptions she knew of.

''How's Albert working out? Have you seen him lately?'' Cleo asked to change the conversation.

She shrugged her shoulders. ''I don't know. We live in the same building and he hasn't invited me over yet. Does that make sense to you?''

''So invite yourself over,'' Cleo offered.

''He says his mother rests a lot and doesn't like to be disturbed.''

''It's not like you're going to be as noisy as children,'' Cleo said, leaving the vacuum to run the duster over the shelves. One good thing, once the carpentry was through, they won't have to dust as often.

''You'd think he'd want to . . .'' Rosebud stopped and ducked her head.

''To what?'' Cleo asked, dusting forgotten.

''Well to at least make out. He hasn't made any advances. I wonder if he's gay and there's another man stashed in his apartment.''

''There goes your imagination again. Why bother with you if he's gay?''

''He could be bisexual,'' she continued stubbornly. ''There's something wrong. I just can't put my finger on it.''

''Are you ready for intimacy with him?'' Cleo asked wondering how long she'd wait if Taylor approached her.

''No. But it's unnatural not to even mention it.''

''Perhaps he senses that you aren't ready for him,'' Cleo resumed her dusting. ''Take your time with this one, Rosebud. Don't rush into anything, you know?'' Albert didn't sound very promising. "Sometimes men like to take their time. It's ego deflating to get turned down."

"Maybe you're right. Well, enough about me. What about you? It's about time you found somebody. I have more luck than you, girl."

"Yes, well, Taylor doesn't seem to be taking the hint. It's not like I meet that many eligible men you know, at least not any who appeal to me the way Taylor does."

"You had lunch today."

"He was ready to run off to a fast-food place with a packed lunch bag in his hands."

Rosebud shook her head and laughed. "I don't know about him."

"I know, I know."

"There's something to be said for taste, but if you really want him, I can mix something up for you."

"No thank you. I'll just go the natural route and see what happens."

"When are you getting that Jacuzzi you keep talking about?" she asked cautiously.

"After the shop is finished and the grand opening," Cleo smiled at the thought.

"Somebody's got to install it, don't they?" she said carefully.

Cleo wondered what she was up to.

"Uh huh." Cleo was suspicious.

"Get Taylor to do it."

Cleo looked up at Rosebud. "I thought you didn't trust him."

She shrugged her shoulders. "I don't know. Maybe I'm being overcautious. To think of it, he couldn't be any worse than Albert. And it would get you to do something other than work, which is all you do now," Rosebud admonished.

"While he's there, you can put some jasmine and clary sage in your diffuser fan. That should get him in the mood. May do more than put in that tub."

"I'll settle for getting to know him better first, thank you." The thought of sharing that Jacuzzi with Taylor had her heartbeat accelerating.

"There's getting to know and there's getting to *know*. You catch my meaning?"

"For an old lady you can be fresh."

"Who are you calling old? This lady's got more moves left in her than you ever thought of."

Cleo laughed because she knew Rosebud was right. She would ask Taylor to put in the Jacuzzi for her. The job in the shop was almost through.

"Be careful though. I still don't quite trust him. He could prove me wrong. Just, take it slow."

Cleo finally started the vacuum. The shop was so tiny. Soon she'd have the new and airy space to greet her guests. Just in time to greet the busiest shopping season of the year.

Since Taylor was between jobs, he might be willing to stay on for a while until he found another position. Else she'd have to hire more people for the holiday season. Keeping Taylor longer would give her more time to work on him.

If she sensed that he didn't like her, she wouldn't pursue him, but sometimes when he thought she wasn't looking, he'd give her that smoldering look that said he wanted to pursue her more. And she certainly didn't miss his glazed eyes this afternoon while he watched her V.

Perhaps he'd been hurt in the past. Some men were reluctant to start a new relationship after going through a harrowing one. Taylor didn't strike her like one who'd give up.

She'd have to stop forcing her traits on others. Just because she was tenacious didn't mean everyone was. She could settle for a more laid-back type. As long as he wasn't too easygoing. Then, too, he worked for her. Conceivably, he was reluctant to mix his personal life with business.

Taylor stood at the aft deck looking across the marina. As the tides rose and the brisk wind whipped his wind-breaker, he popped the cap on his Bud.

He couldn't imagine a better setting to soothe his soul than the sunset this evening or the rippling water.

The only thing better would be to cast off to a secluded cove and put down anchor. There, he'd put out a fishing pole and spend the day. The water, the fish, trees, blue sky, and him—alone.

Having spent the last few years moonlighting as a carpenter to save for his Sea Ray sport yacht, Taylor thought he could finally put the hard labor behind him and settle in his job as postal inspector.

Instead, he was working undercover—as a carpenter again—investigating Cleopatra's Aromatherapy.

Taylor rotated his shoulders. He'd put in extra hours, working into the night to get the shop ready in time.

He moved to the chair and sank into it to watch the sunset. Within minutes, the brisk wind had picked up even more, but he didn't care. To him, the refreshing wind whipped away the worries of the day.

He turned at hearing someone approach, knowing it was Sam. Security had called him for permission to let him enter the marina.

"Permission to board?" Sam said laughing with a smart salute.

"Denied." Taylor felt reluctant to have his peace interrupted. "Come aboard," he said grudgingly. Couldn't the man at least let him enjoy the setting sun?

The boat barely swayed when Sam stepped aboard. Taylor liked the gentle sway on the bay. Friends kept asking him why he rented out his town house. The living quarters on his boat were cramped in comparison. Anything he didn't need to live was packed in storage and Taylor realized he didn't miss any of the items.

One day he would move back into his town house. But for now he could enjoy the water, the smell of the bay he loved, on his small cabin cruiser.

It was good for unwinding after a day of smelling Cleo's sexy perfume and seeing her bright smile when she came bearing tea ten times a day.

"Want a beer?" he asked Sam.

"Coffee would be better."

Hating to leave the deck, Taylor rose and dropped the plastic that winterized the yacht.

"Let's talk inside," Taylor said, turning to enter the cabin.

It was warm and toasty inside. He shucked his jacket, laying it across the couch as he went to start the coffee brewing, indicating to Sam to follow suit.

As soon as it perked, he poured a cup for Sam and

set it on the L-shaped dinette. At least he could glimpse
the last of the setting sun.

Sam sipped on his coffee and sighed. "Any progress?"

"Nothing that says she's involved in fraud. I searched
her computer files and found letters stating she was
returning their checks and asked the women to consult
their families and physicians for medical advice. Can't
go to court with that," he said.

"Protection," Sam said as he leaned back in his chair.
The cruiser rocked with a gust of wind and Sam looked
startled.

Taylor shrugged. This tiny movement was barely a
pitch and sway at all. Taylor wondered what the man
would do in a real gully washer.

"We need concrete evidence and fast," Taylor said.
"Rosebud is very suspicious of me. She watches me like
a hawk." He leaned forward for his beer and took a
long swallow of the cold brew. The taste wrapped itself
around his taste buds. Yeah, this was the life. He'd soon
get Sam out of here and unwind.

"Get a subpoena for her bank records," he continued. "See if she has some accounts we aren't aware of.
Perhaps you can follow the accountant for a few days
to see if he's connected to any of this."

"Sure," Sam said. "Even she has to put the money
someplace other than under her mattress."

Even as, in her innocence, she reminded him of a
choir girl on Sunday morning, he thought of the long
lists of names of cases he'd dealt with similar to hers.

"It still boggles my mind that hordes of women flock
to that store for her products, spending lots of hard-
earned money." He popped in and out the shop all the
time. During lunch and after work it was busy, and

many times all three of the women were busting their backsides waiting on customers. There must have been at least twenty women crowded in that shop around six this afternoon when he'd grabbed a sandwich for dinner.

It hadn't gone unnoticed to Taylor that all the customers were greeted with kind smiles and help when they needed it. More help than he got when he went shopping. Sometimes salesclerks acted as if they were doing customers a favor just by being there, instead of the other way around. He remembered Cleo's conversation with Tina. Perhaps a kind smile could bring customers back over and over to buy worthless products.

"If you can get away with it," Sam said.

"Yeah." Sometimes Taylor thought he was in the wrong business. He needed to come up with a racket. Not for the first time, he thought he could come up with something and retire on easy street in a few years.

Taylor thought of the people who continued to spend thousands on mail-order rackets and knew he could never make his money that way and sleep at night. Every day people spent money over and over on useless products through these scams, and as soon as postal inspectors hit one sight, they'd already moved to another location.

He couldn't catch them all, but Taylor *would* catch Cleopatra Sharp, if it was the last thing he did! He gave a silent salute to Sam and the night.

Chapter 4

Wearing slim wool dark beige slacks and a teal sweater with pearls, and her hair blowing in the wind, Cleo directed the UPS driver as he carried boxes into her shop. Her nose had started to redden from the cold.

Unseen, Taylor gazed out the bank of windows, taking his fill of her. Her verve and energetic steps made her a pleasure to watch. She'd tucked her hair behind her ear to keep it out of her eyes. Today, she wore discreet pearl earrings. Looking at the pants, Taylor thought it was too bad she hadn't worn a full skirt.

He listened to their conversation as they neared the storage room. "The order arrived a day before I expected it to," Cleo said as she directed the driver to stack the boxes by the storage room door.

Hastily she shifted boxes off the scarred tables, transferring them onto the stacks of other boxes in the storage room.

In an effort to be more accommodating and cordial, Taylor went in to assist her. Besides, it was a shame to get those slacks dirty.

"Orders for the open house will be coming in fast and furious," Cleo said to him as he moved boxes. "Besides, I got a large order from Bay Hotel chain, which means I have to hire packers to get everything out in time," she continued happily dragging a box across the room.

"Hotel?" Taylor asked.

"Yes. My biggest mail orders are from companies wanting to give baskets for Christmas and salons who use the products for massages. Hotels like my special soaps and shampoos for corporate guests."

The dangerous image of a massage with her long fingers stroking his skin sprang forth.

"Um," he responded, grunting under the weight of the box he lifted. He didn't know if the grunt was from the box or the image of a massage from her.

He noticed the excitement building in her and realized she always got excited at the prospect of new business.

He wondered how excited she'd get in bed.

"Some of these will be arranged into gift boxes for the holiday season," she laughed, a catch in her breath. She didn't care how many people she had to employ as long as business was brisk.

"I'm almost through with this. Do you need some extra help for the holidays?" He'd gathered zilch so far. Without something else to do, he'd be out of here in a week, Taylor realized.

"Yes, I do." Seeming relieved somehow, she gazed at him. "Would you mind working in the shop, or helping with the mail orders?"

"Not at all." He hoped his half smile didn't look too eager or resemble a satisfied smirk.

"I wanted to talk to you about another project. . . ." She stopped as the UPS man shoved a clipboard at her. She signed the form and thanked him.

Cleo turned back to Taylor where they both stood at the doorjamb. "I want to install a Jacuzzi in my house, but the bathroom is too small to accommodate it. I want to hire you to knock out a couple of walls to enlarge the bath and install the Jacuzzi. It's a major undertaking.''

"Sure. I could do that in the evenings and weekends." Just the excuse he needed to get in her house and snoop around, Taylor thought.

Cleo's smile brought the sunshine inside the shop. Taylor sucked in a breath and wondered, as he returned to his work and her essence remained with him, if he was slowly stepping into her radiant heat.

That afternoon Taylor met Sam at the office. The man plopped a copy of a canceled check on Taylor's desk, dropped into the chair to wait for his reaction.

Taylor picked it up. It was made out to Cleopatra's Aromatherapy.

"Where did this come from?" Taylor asked, dropping it on the desk.

"One of our complaints. I was just going to interview the woman. She's from Columbia, Maryland," Sam said. "I think I have just enough time to talk to her today."

Taylor stood. "I'll tag along."

"How long ago did this happen?" Taylor asked once they were in the car.

"She got the check two days ago and called the office, dissatisfied with the product."

Taylor pulled into the traffic.

"Finally, something solid." Taylor didn't know if he felt exhilaration or apprehension with the news. It was time they got something solid. Being around her was tugging at his—heart? Thinking of this woman diminished his attraction.

It must be something else, he assured himself as he

drove with Sam along 95 North. They were just ahead of the rush-hour traffic, passing several vehicles that had been stopped by police officers beside the road.

In no time they were taking the Columbia exit. The planned suburban community sported clean, quiet streets. Mrs. Carp lived in a well-kept town house development that must have been at least twenty years old.

Sam looked at his paper to determine the house number. It was located on a quaint cul-de-sac. Tall trees were just beginning to shed. The gold, brown, and orange leaves reflected the earth-toned colors of the buildings.

Mrs. Carp greeted them at the door. Her warm smile brightened Taylor's laconic mood. Backing back, shoulders slightly stooped, Mrs. Carp moved aside, letting Taylor and Sam enter the town house.

Pristine white French sofas covered in plastic held several satin floral pillows.

"Have a seat please," Mrs. Carp said. She perched in a chair across from them.

The woman probably spent the better part of the week dusting all the tables filled with sundry knick-knacks. Every surface was filled with small photographs.

"May I get you some of my homemade lemonade? I made it just this morning," she asked.

"Thank you," Taylor said. Mrs. Carp happily rose to get the beverage.

"I've been here for twenty-five years," she said. "Many of my neighbors are still here, too."

Over the fireplace mantle, Taylor perused picture frames covering the wooden surface. They ranged from babies to senior citizens. In the center, a picture of a man in an Army uniform with his arm around someone who must have been a younger Mrs. Carp captured

Taylor's eye. He got up and glided to the mantle for a better view.

"That's my Richard," she said as she came in bearing two glasses of iced lemonade, each with a slice of lemon. "That was just before he went overseas. He fought in the Korean War." A loving smile caressed the picture.

"You must have married young."

"At eighteen. Right out of high school." Her eyes warmed, then saddened. "We were married two weeks before Richard left to go to Korea. "He . . . ," She cleared her throat. "He passed away three months ago."

Taylor placed the frame back on the mantle and returned to his seat. Mrs. Carp placed the lemonade on a coaster on the cocktail table. He took a sip, pleased it was homemade, delicious, and not too sweet, but perfectly tart and lemony. Just the way he liked it.

Mrs. Carp reminded Taylor of his grandmother. Seeming frail, yet unbending strength structured her character and bearing. He still remembered how much she'd hated having to leave her home to move in with his family when her health began to fail. The once vivacious woman who'd always had loving arms and a warm smile had withered before his eyes. She wanted to be in her own home where she'd lived since she married.

"Mrs. Carp," Taylor finally said as he set his glass back on the coaster. "I understand you've lost money from Cleopatra's Aromatherapy."

"It was for my husband. He became very ill with cancer. I got a call that said she had the cure for it. It didn't help at all and I spent so much money." She wiped her eyes as tears slipped past her lids. She looked up at Taylor, anger darting from her eyes.

"Why would they lie like that about something so crucial. How can they get away with it?" She balled her hands into fists on her lap.

"That's why we're here, Mrs. Carp. We're trying to catch the people responsible for this. I understand you have canceled checks of your transaction."

"Yes I do." She rose and walked across the room and pulled out a drawer. She pulled the canceled checks out and handed them to him.

Four checks, five-thousand dollars each. The checks were made out to Cleopatra's Aromatherapy, the handwriting resembled the scrawl he'd become familiar with the last few weeks—that of Cleo's but without something to compare it to, he couldn't be sure.

Still, where was the connection to her backers? Taylor wondered. Unconsciously, he'd been hoping that he'd been wrong about her. That she wasn't dealing in fraud after all.

Cleo put several drops of peppermint in the aromatherapy fan and switched it on. Immediately, the fresh, invigorating scent curled up to her nose, soon permeating the entire shop. She had two hours before the doors would open for the day. Rosebud would be in to help her put together gift baskets soon, she knew.

She was especially ecstatic because the wallpaper would go up in the addition today and they'd start the busy task of arranging items in the new section.

After brewing a pot of tea, she started on the gift baskets. Most people would dread a job they thought was mundane, but Cleo loved making beautiful things.

In the first group of baskets, she arranged a silk eye

pillow with scented body lotion, body shampoo, bath salts, soap, and a candle, sealing it with the clear yellow cellophane and adding a gold bow for the finishing touch.

She'd completed ten baskets before Rosebud came bustling in shaking her umbrella.

"How was your hot date last night?" Cleo asked her, always enjoying her tales.

"That man has the most clinging mother I've ever encountered," she moaned as she sat at the table, the humidity causing her dyed light brown hair to curl up tighter although it still looked very pretty along with her attractive face.

"She's not ready to give him up yet?" Cleo asked.

"I can't come over because it might disturb her. So I invited him over to my place. Candlelit dinner. Thought we'd get romantic." She disappeared into the storage room. "He brings his mom to dinner," she continued as she reemerged and flopped on a chair.

Cleo laughed. "He didn't!"

"You can laugh, but it isn't funny at all. Not that I mind inviting her. I just wanted to spend the evening alone with him." She grabbed a basket and started packing.

"He did return after he escorted her home, didn't he? After all, they're upstairs from you, not in the next town."

"Are you kidding?" Rosebud waved a hand.

"Perhaps you should forget about him."

"He's so nice, you know. When he does come over, we talk easily about everything—current events, politics, crime—come to think of it, we don't discuss personal issues, just . . . I'm coming to the conclusion he'll just be a friend.''

"Sometimes that's enough. You don't have to have an affair with every man you meet.''

"True. We even like the same music.''

"He can't be all bad then,'' Cleo joked.

"He's not. It's just . . . I don't know. I don't want to sound hard or unkind toward his mother, but why would she do that to a son?''

"She could be lonely. If she doesn't have other friends, he probably keeps the loneliness at bay.''

"You'd think she'd want grandchildren. She can't do that for him.''

"At fifty, I don't think he wants children, Rosebud.''

"He could already have children. Men can be secretive about certain things.''

"Which wouldn't speak highly of his character.''

"I'm sure he doesn't. His mom controls him too much.''

"Enough about me, already. Tell me about Taylor. Lord, girl. You could almost cut the air that steams around you two.''

"He doesn't take the hint.'' Cleo sighed. "At least he talks to me now. He only grunted before.''

Rosebud paused. "Didn't you say he agreed to fix your bathroom for you?''

"Yes. But that's work.''

"There's work and there's *work*. I told you what to do to get him. Have some oysters and wine for dinner.'' Rosebud waved a bottle of jasmine. "Before he leaves, he'll be yours.'' She leaned back laughing at her own ingeniousness.

Cleo laughed with her. "The attraction has to be mutual for it to work, you know."

"Take it from me. It is. I don't know why you want him. And I certainly don't trust him. But, at least he's someone to pass the lonely hours with until something better comes along. Almost like Albert." She frowned as she picked up a bottle of lotion. "At least he puts in a good day's work. More than you can say for some. Of course I keep wondering why he hasn't found another job yet."

"I got glowing recommendations," Cleo reminded her. "And you can't complain about the quality of his work."

"That's what I mean. A man in a technical field who's good at his job shouldn't be jobless for long. Don't you find that strange?"

"It takes longer than a month to find good jobs. I'm sure he doesn't want to settle for just anything. It all takes time. I'm lucky he's here."

"All right, all right."

Rosebud was from the school that said if he kept a job, there had to be something good about him.

The phone rang. Cleo dropped the bow she was in the process of tying and ran to her office.

"Good morning," she said.

"Hello, is this Cleopatra Sharp?" the voice asked.

"Yes, it is. How may I help you?" Cleo responded, leaning a hip against the desk.

"I'm Margaret Patterson. I received your letter yesterday asking me to call you about the cancer medicine," she stated hesitantly.

"Oh, thank you for responding, Mrs. Patterson. Cleopatra's Aromatherapy doesn't sell cures for terminal illness. I was wondering how you got my name.''

"I got a call from you saying you'd gotten my name from some insurance database that kept track of certain types of cancer. That my husband was the perfect candidate for your cure. It had helped thousands of people before."

"And they gave you my address?"

"Let me check, because I lost the address but I remembered the name. I had my friend who got a new computer hooked up to that Internet search for your name. She told me everything was there. That's where we found your address. After I mailed it, I found the real address."

"Could you give me that address?" Cleo asked, now whirling around to sit while she grabbed pad and pen.

"Don't you know it?" the woman asked.

"No, I didn't call you. I just need to stop these people from stealing money from people like you. There aren't any special or secret cures."

"That's just horrible!" the woman bellowed in outrage.

"Yes, it is. That's why I need your help to stop them." Cleo held the pen impatiently above the pad.

"Give me a minute," she said. "I'm so glad I lost that address. I would have lost thousands otherwise."

Cleo snatched the phone from her ear when she heard a loud clang.

"Sorry about that," Mrs. Patterson said. "I'll be right back."

Cleo waited and waited wondering what her next step would be.

"Here it is," Mrs. Patterson's winded voice

announced. She rattled off an address in Germantown, Maryland. "Thank you so much. I hope you're reporting this to the authorities."

"Yes, I am."

"Thank you so much," Cleo said. "And please listen to your doctor's advice." The woman thanked Cleo and they parted.

Progress. Cleo smiled then frowned.

She was marching toward the door when she realized it was time to open the store.

Germantown was more than an hour away. She couldn't make it there and back before the lunch rush. Cleo sighed impatiently and put the slip of paper into her purse. As soon as Tina—Tina was off today. She balled her fist in frustration. She'd find a way to get there today. Perhaps at two when business slowed, she thought.

Chapter 5

"Sam?" Taylor carried his voice louder than normal. He had intentionally picked the busiest time for Cleo to make the call to his partner so Cleo, or especially Rosebud, wouldn't notice his absence.

"Yeah?"

"This is my first break all day. Let's make it quick." Taylor stood looking around him at the gas station pay phone. The battery was dead in his cell phone.

The roar of traffic on Oxen Hill Road left him holding a hand to his other ear to hear Sam's voice.

"We've found one of the mailboxes and put a watch on it. Got a subpoena for it and checked the mail. The box is signed in Ms. Sharp's name, but it's not her signature, though it's a close forgery."

"Rosebud's?" Taylor asked, annoyed at dead-end after dead-end.

"We compared it with hers but it wasn't hers either."

"Where's the box?"

"In Germantown."

"They could have hired anyone to open the box. If only we could catch them at something. All we have are names and forgeries." Taylor switched feet. "We need to find out if someone's working with her. If we don't stop them, they'll just move to a new location and use someone else. I'll try to snoop in her house."

"Business as usual."

It was harder and harder to think of Cleo's involvement. When he thought of her effervescent personality, he wished there was something he could do for her. He knew all too well what excessive greed could do to a person. That greed could twist a soul so much that hard work, and a steady inflow of cash wouldn't be enough to appease them. They'd want even more, not caring that they hurt others. And what could he do about that?

Absolutely nothing.

Taylor hardened his resolve. Cleopatra was a grown woman and an entrepreneur. She was fully capable of making her own decisions. Some inner voice nagged that she'd have to live with it if she was guilty.

"It's a good cover for when she's caught. I can see

it now, 'Your honor, it's her name, her business, her mailbox, but not her signature.' It'll get thrown out of court before our butts can warm the seats." Taylor sighed.

"Isn't this a . . ." Sam muttered an oath under his breath as a truck sailed past Taylor.

"You know, Sam, someone could be impersonating her." Taylor heard Sam pause and knew he took a drag on his cigarette.

"I doubt it, but . . ." Sam responded.

"Yeah, well, it's too soon to tell."

"It's the weekend and we need a few more days to work with this. Just stick close to her. After she graduated from college, she spent a few years in London. If she gets an inkling that we're watching her, she might skip the country again," he said worriedly.

"Sure." Taylor wondered if this business with the Jacuzzi was a ruse to make anyone watching her think she had long-term plans here while she was scheming something big, and leaving before they could close in on her.

Taylor didn't know what to believe, except that if she was savvy enough to start an aromatherapy business from scratch, create her own product brands, and make a success of the business, then she was certainly intelligent enough to try to pull off this mail-fraud scheme.

But why would she want to, after laying down roots in Maryland? The shop wasn't portable. And damn if she didn't work harder than most two people.

Was she a criminal mastermind or an innocent victim? Only time would tell.

"All the accounts you gave us are legitimate. Just regular credits and debits in line with her kind of business. The only large checks were from bigger companies for large orders.'' Sam said.

Taylor wondered again if someone was impersonating her. It happened every day. People stole credit cards statements and loans, changed the address on the forms, ran up debits and months later, credit departments hunted the original owner down to collect on delinquent bills only to find out it wasn't that person after all.

That still left the question of who was forging her name—and why? Why choose Cleopatra Sharp? Although an aromatherapy business where she worked with all kinds of oils, along with being a chemistry major, made her perfect for the fraud if anyone wanted to set her up.

He wondered who her enemies were. Had she angered a boyfriend? Had she whisked a man from some spiteful woman? All kinds of possibilities came to mind.

If she wasn't guilty, she was the perfect patsy to keep the postal inspectors busy while the guilty party continued to reap in the rewards.

Still, it was too soon to eliminate her completely.

"I'm coming in this afternoon," he told Sam as a bread truck hit the brakes and barely missed hitting a Mustang.

His carpentry work at Cleopatra's Aromatherapy was basically done, except for a few touch-ups he'd make after the wallpaper hangers finished today.

Tonight he'd be working in her house.

After his trip to the pay phone, Taylor returned to the shop to pack gift baskets with Ashand and his football buddy, Bertrand. He was surprised to see the bulky teenagers, whose large hands handled delicate items with finesse and skill. He noticed Ashand's graceful fingers were testament of his position on the football field.

Their clothes were the usual teenage attire. The ever-present baggy jeans. Although Ashand's were baggy, his seat stayed in the proper place. As large as he was, the seat of Bertrand's pants hit at mid thigh. Both had loose-fitting T-shirts for covering. Ashand wore a generic brand while Bertrand wore Polo.

"Oh, man, we really whipped Carver, didn't we?" Ashand said.

"That ball just slid in my hand like it was made for me," Bertrand returned, his eyes glassy. He threw up a bottle of lotion and deftly caught it.

This is one big dude, Taylor thought. He wouldn't want to be in his way on a football field.

The phone rang and startled them, Bertrand almost dropped the glass bottle he held. Taylor thought someone that big wouldn't fear very much, especially a phone that rang constantly.

"So, how do you guys keep fit in the summer? Do you work out in school?" Taylor asked, stuffing jasmine body wash in a basket.

"No, I do some part-time work at Hillside Gym. They let me use the equipment as part of the benefits. Doesn't pay much. I sneak Ashand in." Bertrand handed Taylor the lotion and shampoo to match.

"How long have you worked for Cleo?" Taylor asked. Wrapping the paper around the package, he handed the package for Ashand to put on the bow.

"We started last year after Tina started working here." He made the prettiest bow Taylor had seen.

"We can't work every day because of football," Bertrand said.

"We do her special packing, if it's not too much. For really big orders she hires a group from the church," Ashand continued.

"So you and Tina are going to open your own Victoria's Secret?" Taylor asked.

"That's what Tina wants," Ashand said, clearly satisfied with the plans. "We're saving money out of each of our paychecks for it now."

"Is that what you want?" Taylor asked.

"Yeah. At first I'll work another job while Tina gets the lingerie business started. I'll do the accounting though. When we can afford it, I'll quit and work with Tina. We want to open a chain of shops," Ashand said and Taylor thought Ashand and Tina's relationship had an excellent chance of surviving college, after all.

"I like to see young people who set goals and develop the plans to achieve them. I'm proud of you."

Ashand smiled in embarrassment. "Tina's wanted a store since kindergarten."

"Does Cleo plan to open chains of aromatherapy shops?" Taylor cautiously asked.

"No. She likes hands-on control. She can't do that with several shops."

It also meant putting in stronger roots in the area. He realized she didn't hang out with friends often.

"What are your plans, Bertrand?"

"I wanna go pro."

With his build, Taylor knew he had a better than average chance of making it.

"That's why I'm going to Grambling," Bertrand continued. "Coach is the best at training."

"I agree," Taylor said. "What will you two major in?"

"Accounting," Ashand said.

"Physical education," Bertrand said. "If I don't go pro, I'll teach. Cleo told me I needed to be prepared just in case." He handed Taylor more lotion.

There it goes again. Her positive influence on kids, Taylor thought.

"Why don't you come to one of our games?" Ashand asked. "Homecoming's coming up in a week."

"I just might do that," Taylor responded, thinking that it would give him a good opening with Cleo. A game was innocent enough.

"And bring Cleo," Ashand added.

Taylor laughed.

"I'm serious man. You got a main squeeze?"

Taylor almost didn't answer the personal question. But he realized the young man was just trying to be friendly. "Not at the moment."

"Good. Cleo's okay for somebody her age."

Taylor felt ancient.

"Come early before the tickets sell out. You can get them at the gate or I can pick them up for you. They may sell out so you should get them early."

"How much are they?"

Ashand named a price. Taylor reached in his pocket for his billfold and handed Ashand the money for two tickets.

"I've been looking for a place to workout. How are the hours at Hillside?"

"It's great man. From six to eleven at night."

"And it's near here," Ashand added. "You can go after you get off work."

"I'll drop by next week."

"Let me know when you're coming. They give me a commission for bringing you in, even though sales isn't my thing."

"I will," Taylor said.

Cleo bustled in, hurried as if she couldn't wait to leave. Still, seeing her was like a ray of sunshine.

Suddenly Taylor realized how much he looked forward to seeing her burst in on him with a warm smile and a hot cup of tea. Once he left, he'd miss her.

"How is it going in here?" The green of her blouse next to her face made her seem vibrant and cheerful.

"Going right along," Bertrand said. "Taylor said he's bringing you to the homecoming game."

"Oh?" She raised an eyebrow as she glanced at Taylor. "He didn't mention that to me."

"He just handed me the money to buy the tickets," Ashand said.

Taylor cleared his throat. "I hadn't gotten around to asking you yet."

"What are you waiting for man?" Bertrand asked, "Go ahead. Ask her."

"Hey, can't you let me do it my way?" Taylor said, embarrassed.

Both the boys stopped working and looked at him. "Well?" They rolled their eyes.

Taylor sighed. "Would you like to attend the Homecoming game next Friday night with me? If you can get off, that is," he asked with amusement.

"Oh, man. You're really behind the times. Who talks like that any more?"

"I accept," Cleo quickly replied amid the boys' ribbing.

"Good," Ashand said. "Gonna be a good one. We're playing against Carver again."

"Man, we really gotta work on you," cut in Bertrand. "You'll never keep a woman with a line like that. Loosen up some, will you." He slapped Taylor on the back, and even at six-four Taylor almost toppled.

Face heating from Ashand and Bertrand's ribbing, Taylor said, "I'll do my best."

"So man, where's home? You can't be from around here talking like that."

"Georgia."

"Yeah? What part? You go to private school or something?" Bertrand wanted to know.

"Atlanta, Catholic school even though I'm Baptist." The packing started again.

"You really had it tough, didn't you?"

Taylor thought of the strict nuns and all the trouble he stayed in. Corporal punishment was still practiced at that time. "It wasn't easy." Still, he'd gotten a good education. And it definitely kept him in line.

"You don't have the typical southern accent."

"I left home twelve years ago. Picked up a new accent."

"Dress warm, Cleo," Ashand warned. "It's going to be a cool night out there."

"I will. It hasn't been that long since I've been to a game, you know. I played basketball in high school," she said not looking the type at all.

"Were you any good?"

"The best."

Taylor tried to picture this graceful woman charging up and down the court but couldn't.

She glanced at Taylor.

"Are you still coming by the house tonight?" she asked Taylor hesitantly.

"Will seven do?" That was three hours away.

She glanced at her watch. "Seven will be fine. I'm leaving in a few minutes, but Rosebud will be here." She pulled a slip of paper out her pocket. "Here's my address and directions to my house."

Taylor followed the sway of her hips as she left the room and ignored the ribbing from the boys.

After perusing a map for directions to Here Today Mail Boxes, Cleo charged out of her shop and was soon heading north on the Beltway. She left early knowing she wouldn't get a minute's sleep tonight if she didn't check out that box.

It took more than an hour—speeding—to get there. It was located in a quaint shopping plaza with a Giant grocery store, Kmart, and a variety of shops in between. Cleo pulled into the closest parking space.

She marched up to the box as if she had a right to be there. The store was busy and the clerks harried.

Cleo glimpsed the many signs sporting their services. They mailed FedEx as well as UPS, sold cards, gift wrappings, and faxed. An all-in-one stop, Cleo thought.

When it was her turn, on the off chance the box was in her name, she said, "Suite 135 belongs to me, but I've misplaced my key. Would it be possible to get another one?" She honored the harried clerk with a dazzling smile.

He sighed as if to say, that's the last thing he needed today. "Yes, but you need identification and you'll have to pay for it," he said as the line of people behind her waited impatiently.

Cleo whipped out her driver's license and handed it to him. He went over to the computer and looked up something. Then he went into the back room and in a few minutes bought back a key.

"It's been so long since anyone's been to that box, we've got some of the mail stored in back." He brought a huge bag out to her.

"Thank you."

"You'll have to bring the bag back though."

"Will tomorrow be okay?" she asked.

"Sure."

Lugging the bag, Cleo went to the box and opened it. It was filled to the brim.

First she looked at the names on the envelopes. Her stomach hit rock bottom.

Every letter was addressed to Cleopatra's Aromatherapy.

Sighing, Cleo dug out the rest of the mail and shoved it in the bag with the others and all but dragged it to her car.

Once there, she leaned her elbow on the steering wheel. This wasn't something she could handle on her own. Since the mail was made out to her, she opened a letter. It had a check for ten thousand in it. She tore open another one. It had a check for twenty thousand.

She read one of the letters. The owner stated she'd cleaned house and scrubbed floors for years to save up her money.

Cleo wondered why people let themselves be duped so easily out of their hard-earned money.

Twenty thousand was a lifetime earnings for someone

who scrubbed floors all their lives and saved bit-by-bit. What kind of evil resided in one to even consider stealing from them?

You're in big trouble, she said to herself. This wasn't some ordinary person playing a prank. They were hardened criminals.

Cleo drove slowly back to her house and carted the bag in dumping the letters into a huge black garbage bag.

On the way home, she'd decided she'd have to hire a lawyer. If she went to the police now, they'd haul her behind in jail before she could say "pass go."

A quick glance at her watch told her she had a mere half hour before Taylor would arrive. She wasn't in the mood for Jacuzzis or bathrooms.

She also knew she couldn't let this change her plans. For the next few months, she'd need every pick-me-up she could get.

Chapter 6

Taylor drove through an old neighborhood with Tudors, colonials, split-levels, and ranch houses. Some were as large as mini mansions, others were smaller two-bedroom duplexes.

Cleo's brick rambler was tucked back in a nest of trees and shrubs near the end of a small cul-de-sac. A few flowers struggled to survive. The grass at least was cut, but scattered brown patches cried out for fungicide.

Taylor could determine immediately she didn't lavish the care on her yard that she applied to her shop. He knew she didn't have time left to spend on yard work.

He parked in front of her garage door and walked the cobblestone path to her door. The house looked to have been built during the fifties, was sturdy, and well-maintained.

When the rose mixed with something else hit him as soon as Cleo opened the door, Taylor wrinkled his nose.

She'd changed into black stretch pants, wearing a loose mauve V-neck shirt over it. Taylor had difficulty taking his eyes off her legs, but he did notice that her hair was swept up to show her delicious neck.

"Hi, come on in." She moved back so he could pass. A frown puckered her brow. Absentmindedly, she rubbed her forehead.

Taylor recalled that she'd been more preoccupied than usual today. He'd put it down to the rush from the grand opening, but he wondered if it was something else altogether.

Passing her, he caught a whiff of her perfume. Smelling fresh from the shower, her skin glowed. The only makeup she used was lipstick.

He stepped into the foyer, observing the living room on his left. He didn't quite know what he'd expected, but from the decor of her shop he pictured something tasteful and eye-catching. He wasn't disappointed.

The basic color scheme revolved around blue. The stuffed chairs weren't new, but were covered in ice-blue fabric with print pillows. A painting of the buffalo soldiers hung behind the couch, the darker blue in the uniform a sharp contrast to the ice-blue couch. Were it not for the pillows and accoutrements in the room, it would be cold. But all her unique touches made the room as cozy as a roaring fire.

"The bathroom is back here." She strutted ahead of him, giving him little time to glimpse the family room with its huge stone fireplace covering the entire wall. Then she stopped short.

"I'm sorry. Can I get you something to eat or drink?" she asked, as an afterthought.

At her sudden stop, he almost bumped into her. "Nothing, thanks."

"Maybe after you take a look?"

"Fine."

They passed two small bedrooms, one she used as an office with a neat little stack of papers on the desk and open letters scattered about. The mailbag beside it caught Taylor's interest. And this was after he believed she was innocent.

It seemed as if something died in Taylor at seeing that bag. Here lay the mail he'd been searching for. He still wondered who opened the account for her and who usually retrieved the mail.

He scarcely noticed the rest of the house. On the other side of the hall, he passed a small bath, the smallest bedroom, and then arrived at the master suite. It looked to be fifteen by fifteen.

The blue color scheme from the living room followed to the bedroom, though it was warmer, with the mauve and ivory pattern in the bedspread, carpeting, pillows, candles, and other areas in the room.

Light spilled from antique lamps on each side of the brass bed. Blue shades covered the large picture window. Taylor knew when they were opened during the day, they bathed the room in light.

Candles were placed on the dresser and tables. Taylor marveled at the romantic setting they made. A setting he'd never appreciate now that the proof of her duplicity was down the hall in her office.

He longed for an opportunity to spend time there.

Cleo opened a door. "As you see, this bath is much too small for a Jacuzzi. I'd like to tear everything out of here and use most of the bedroom next door for the bath and the rest of that room used to enlarge the other bath."

The tiny bath had a small shower, commode, and sink. Today, developers built much larger master baths.

She handed him a sheet of paper. "I made a crude diagram of what I want."

Taylor took the graphing paper. She'd drawn everything to scale. It offered a window view which was missing now. He would need to move some of the plumbing in the room. Which meant she'd be unable to use it.

"Do you have another bathroom you can use while I'm renovating these?" he asked.

"In the basement I have a bath with a shower. On the other side of the kitchen is a half bath. I'll make do with them."

While he looked around she continued to talk. "I've already ordered the Jacuzzi. I wanted to wait for you before I bought the shower and everything else, but I know what I want."

"After I take some measurements, we can look at the fixtures you're interested in. Then I'll work up a quote." He took out a pencil and made notations on the diagram.

"Sounds good."

He took out his tape measure and started on the measurements. The room was small, but clean. All the fixtures were very old and in need of sprucing up. But overall, the building was sturdy and would last much longer than the models built today.

Taylor was facing the door when Cleo passed the room. For a moment he forgot what he was doing. He remembered something about Cleopatra, queen of Egypt, walking through rose petals for her bath, and her sensuous nature and effect on men. He wondered if the rose he was smelling was having a similar effect on him.

And he couldn't afford to let that happen.

"Are you ready to go for supplies?"

"Oh, yes." He rolled the tape back, folded up the paper and stuck it with the pen he was using into his pocket. This trip didn't offer the opportunity for him to check around for bank accounts or peek at her letters.

She grabbed a jacket from the closet and preceded him out the door.

Once again, Taylor had a lovely vision as he walked behind her, her pants clinging to every curve.

He also realized he didn't feel like a towering giant with her.

As he checked the doorknob to make sure it was locked, Taylor thought that Cleo didn't live like a woman out for grand riches with a modest four-bedroom house. She'd purchased the house a mere three months ago. Had she expensive tastes, she would have purchased one of more grandeur in an upscale community instead of an older one.

* * *

Taylor didn't make it home until after eleven. He pulled off his hat and grabbed a beer on his way to the bath. As he was about to step into the shower, the phone rang.

"Hello," he answered impatiently.

"It's Sam. Remember the mailboxes we were monitoring?"

"Yeah?" Taylor answered, the air bringing goose bumps on his bare skin.

"Well, your lady went there today."

"I saw a huge bag of mail in her office. I'm not surprised." Taylor sighed.

"I thought they'd moved on. Lucky we decided to monitor it one more day. She came out with a huge bag of mail."

The bottom dropped out of Taylor's stomach. He didn't know what he expected anymore. One thing for sure, she wouldn't need that Jacuzzi in jail.

"We've got a twenty-four hour watch on her now. The U.S. Attorney wants to see if we can catch her accomplices, so he doesn't want to bring her in for questioning yet."

The Jacuzzi, the letters he read in her computer, they were all a ruse. Though this was business, Taylor still felt disappointed.

"Thanks, maybe tomorrow night I'll get a closer look in her house."

"Before too long, we'll have search warrants."

* * *

Cleo put a hand to her chest as she walked into the kitchen where Rosebud was brewing tea. She quickly dropped it hoping the woman wouldn't pick up on her emotions. Rosebud's keen eyesight missed nothing.

"What's wrong with you?" she asked, holding the container of hot water.

"Nothing, why?"

"Give me a break." She poured the water in the teapot, spooned tea leaves into the tea ball and immersed it in the water.

"Taylor asked me out for a date. And he's renovating the bath for me." The smell of peppermint filled the air. "I guess I'm excited about it."

"You and that Jacuzzi. I've never seen anybody sock away so long for something so frivolous."

"I've always wanted one. When I saved for the house I socked a little aside for the Jacuzzi. I bought the house with that in mind." Cleo stashed her lunch in the refrigerator, glad Rosebud accepted the lie.

"Well you deserve it. What are you going to save up for next? You're always saving up for something."

Cleo shrugged. "Just put more in my retirement now that I have the house."

"You've been saving for retirement since your first job. Never seen a sixteen-year-old read so much about retirement and squirrel away so much at that age."

"The earlier the better, I've heard. And that reminds me. You need to save a little more, too. You haven't made an increase since you started working here. And your salary has increased." Cleo didn't have the energy to rush into work this morning. She was content to visit with Rosebud before opening the doors.

"Girl, you've been worrying me to death about that."
She pulled a coffee cake out a plastic bag.

There goes her diet, Cleo thought.

"You don't want to work forever, do you? A simple
two-thousand a year IRA isn't going to be enough. If
you don't take care of it now, you *will* be working forever. Not enough money for medical bills or housing,
much less a simple vacation. You deserve better than
that."

"Okay, okay. You can put fear in anybody. You even
got Tina investing in IRAs and she's just a high-school
student. Not even in college yet." Rosebud blew out a
long breath. "You handle it. Set up the plan and let
me know how much I've got to put away." Rosebud
waved a hand. "Thinking about that gets me confused.
Never did like math in school."

"Rosebud, have you thought about ownership instead
of renting? Maybe a town house or a condo, which is
less upkeep. When you consider your taxes, it'll come
out to the same as renting."

"But then I'll have to worry about fixing things
instead of the landlord."

"You'll also own it one day. All the money you're
spending now goes to someone else, not you."

"I'll think about it. Not another word." Rosebud took
down cups and saucers and poured tea for Cleo and
herself. "So Taylor's finally getting the message, I see.
I don't know what you see in that man. Where's he
taking you?"

"To a high-school football game. I think Ashand and
Bertrand talked him into it."

"Be still my beating heart. He's a real live one, isn't

he? You sure you want him?" Rosebud sank in a chair and delicately sipped her tea.

"All right." Cleo threw up her hands. "So it's not the most romantic date. At least it's a start."

"Some start with a stadium full of horny high-school students hovering in their coats out in the cold." She cut two slices of coffee cake and slid one to Cleo.

"Thanks." Cleo forked a bite, making a mental note to carry a slice to Taylor later.

"This is delicious."

"Made it last night." She cut a small piece with her fork. "What time is he coming over tonight?"

"Around seven."

"If you leave early enough, you can get home in time to set things up. Light some candles. Put on some Luther. Maybe he'll get the message and do better than a football game. Young folks today."

"I can't be too obvious or he'll think I'm running after him."

"Just tell him it's your after-work routine to calm your nerves after a hectic day. You've got to do something to get him moving. Otherwise he'll be up and gone before he even gets the message."

"We'll see." Cleo wished she hadn't said anything.

"I got a call from Ronald yesterday. He wants me to visit him for a month after the holiday rush and January inventory." She diverted her gaze.

Cleo's eyes softened. "Wonderful. You'll love Greece. You have to go."

"I don't know. He doesn't want to marry me and I'm not waiting for him forever," Rosebud said, stubbornness coloring her tone. "I'm not getting any younger."

"Maybe, after missing you, he'll change his mind."
Cleo patted the woman's hand.

"We'll see. Then there's Albert."

"Who you don't like as well as Ronald. And he's a
mama's boy. You have no hopes of forming a lasting
relationship with him."

"These are some pitiful times, aren't they?" Rosebud
sighed and forked up more coffee cake.

Cleo laughed.

Cleo closed her door, marched over to her desk and
flipped through her rolodex as she sat, stopping at
Roland P. James, Esquire. She'd met him at a conference
a year ago. It was just one of the many little numbers
she kept tucked away—just in case.

She dialed and reached his secretary.

"Hello, my name is Cleopatra Sharp. I met Mr. James
a year ago at a Women in Business meeting. I was wondering if I could get an appointment with him today.
It's rather urgent." He was married and tried for a
date that Cleo declined. She'd also gathered from other
women that he was the best at domestic law. She waited
patiently for the secretary to respond.

"You're in luck. He had a cancellation today. He's
available at two."

"I'll be there. Thank you."

Cleo hung up. She relied more and more on Tina
now. She got out of school at one and usually arrived
at the shop by one-thirty. That would give Cleo enough
time to make it to the lawyer's office. Just barely.

Even with her troubles, she still had a business to
run. She was glad for the steady flow of customers, the

impromptu blends she had to make, and the steady phone calls for orders. Otherwise she'd never have made it to one-thirty without biting her nails in nervousness.

She left the shop to Tina and Rosebud.

The offices of James, Stout, and Stout shouted masculine and pricy, with Persian rugs, and lots of mahogany that by its very simplicity bespoke understated luxury.

Perhaps she shouldn't have paid for the bathroom fixtures after all last night. Perhaps she should have waited until all this was over.

The efficient secretary with pretty chestnut hair and clear cinnamon skin, quickly ushered Cleo into his office.

Roland stood as she entered, circling the desk, wearing an Italian-made three-piece suit. His dark complexion coated with virile strength would make the most timid of women yearn for a closer sample of what he had to offer, but Cleo thought she wouldn't want a man like him in a million years. He was much too polished to be real. She'd take her hat off to his wife, who was quite beautiful in her own right, petite with a model-thin build and picture-perfect face.

"It's been a while, Cleo." With his manicured hands, he reached out for her hand. Cleo extended hers for a shake and he held on.

"Yes it has." When he didn't immediately let go, she gave a discreet tug. He patted her hand with the other one before releasing it.

"Have a seat." He tucked a hand in his pocket as he circled his mahogany desk and returned to his butter-soft leather chair.

Cleo sank into the wing chair facing him, eager to get on with business.

"Would you like something to drink? Coffee, tea, soda?" he asked.

"Tea, please." Cleo needed something to still her jumpy stomach.

He reached for the intercom, asking his secretary to bring it in with coffee for him. They made small talk until Cleo had her tea and he took his first sip of coffee. Cleo set her tea on the table beside her.

"What brings you here today?" he finally asked. He picked up his Mont Blanc pen and waited for her response, giving her his undivided attention.

"I'm afraid someone is using my name and my business name to commit fraud. A few weeks ago, I received a twenty-thousand dollar check for a special cancer treatment.

"I returned the check with a letter saying that Cleopatra's Aromatherapy had no special cure and didn't sell medicines or vitamins."

"Was that your only request?" he asked scribbling furiously across the yellow legal pad.

"No, I received about five through my post office box. But last week I enclosed my toll-free number and asked one woman to call me. She called me yesterday and said that she received a letter in the mail advertising that Cleopatra's Aromatherapy had special medication, and because of the expense it wasn't available to everyone.

"She also gave me the box number that she was supposed to use. I tracked it to Here Today Mail Boxes in Germantown. I went there yesterday and told them I had lost my key and asked if I could have another one.

I showed them identification and they gave me a key," Cleo continued.

"The box was in my name and there was an entire bag of mail, all of it made out to Cleopatra's Aromatherapy."

"What did you do with the mail?" Roland finally asked when Cleo paused.

"It's in my car. I opened a few of them. There were thousands of dollars in those envelopes and since I have a whole bag of them, I knew I was in trouble. I've never applied for a box there nor have I advertised special treatments of any kind." Cleo raked a hand through her hair.

"Has anything like this happened to you before?" He continued scribbling across the yellow legal pad.

Cleo explained the incident that occurred in her senior year.

"Did you have a lawyer represent you?" He looked up, his forehead crunched.

"No, it never came to that, but they questioned all the salespeople relentlessly and finally let us go. The owner skipped town and I haven't heard from her since. As far as I know, they weren't caught."

"Do you suspect they're involved in this?" he asked, leveling her with a piercing gaze.

"It would be crazy to come back here." Cleo shifted in her seat.

"Have you contacted the police?" he dulled on as lawyers were known to do.

"No, I haven't. I don't trust them," Cleo said. "I could end up being blamed for this, especially with my background." She shifted in her chair.

He continued writing for a moment. Then he put the pen down, and steepled his fingers.

"We could do two things. First I could write a cease and desist letter to that box and wait for the outcome before following up with the authorities."

"And the other alternative?" Cleo asked not satisfied with that choice.

"Mail fraud is a federal offense handled by the U.S. Attorney's office. I think the better course would be to talk to someone there. I have a contact there who's in the Marine Reserves with me. The conversation would be informal-formal," he said.

"I don't want to go to jail for something I didn't do," Cleo declared.

"It's my job to keep you out of jail. They'll be more agreeable if you cooperate with them and turn that mail over to them. I wouldn't wait on this though."

Cleo wanted the mail off her hands and the process to keep moving forward. "All right. Call your friend," she said with trepidation.

Roland punched a button on the phone. "Barbara. Call Gill Thacher for me in the U.S. Attorney's office, please."

"All right." Cleo heard over the intercom.

"Don't worry." He smiled, full of a lawyer's confidence. "Let me do the worrying for you. That's what you're paying me for."

And a pretty penny, too, Cleo thought. But she always did her own planning and worrying. She wasn't about to stop now no matter how much she trusted him. She declined to answer and merely smiled at him.

The intercom snapped on. "Mr. James?"

"Yes, Barbara?"

"Mr. Thacher on line one."

He picked up the phone. "Gill, how are you?" Roland said leaning forward in his chair.

Unable to sit, Cleo got up and paced around the room, looking at the paintings on the wall as she listened to the one-sided conversation.

"It's been a long time since we've been golfing. Let's get together soon, shall we?" Roland said.

He laughed at a response from Gill.

"I have a client who has some peculiar things happening." He explained the situation.

Roland turned on the intercom at that point.

"Why don't you ask your client to come in to talk to us informally. You know I can't tell you if there's an investigation going on but," Cleo heard some papers rattle. "Your client might be able to assist us in our work."

Roland raised an eyebrow at Cleo.

She nodded yes.

"Let's say tomorrow morning?" Gill said.

Roland consulted his calendar. "Can't do." He mouthed "one" to Cleo.

She nodded.

"How does one sound, Gill?"

"Nothing I can't move to another time. And don't forget the letters."

Roland flipped the speaker off.

Cleo returned to her seat.

"We need a few ground rules. First, anytime I put my hand on your arm, you shut up."

They went though a list of dos and don'ts.

It was another hour before Cleo left, leaving the mail-bag with Roland.

* * *

Dusty from putting the finishing touches on the shop, Taylor ran warm water over his face and hands when he and Sam were summoned to the U.S. Attorney's office late that afternoon. If he were to make it on time, a shower was out of the question.

Gill Thacher, the lead attorney on Cleo's case was six-feet with blond hair. He was known to work out the required three times a week, wore government regulation suits—was politically motivated, high energy, and didn't tackle a case unless he was assured of victory.

Solving the largest mail-fraud scam to hit in years would be a proverbial feather in his cap.

He was quick-witted and one of the sharpest lawyers Taylor had witnessed in a courtroom. He could level his voice to acquire the perfect effect for his audience.

"Gentlemen, today I got a call from a friend who has to be Cleopatra Sharp's attorney. It all fits. He's bringing her in tomorrow for an informal talk." He waited for a reaction.

Taylor barely contained his shock. He wondered if he'd done anything to give Cleo the indication he was investigating her.

When silence greeted the attorney, he continued.

"Evidently she recently discovered someone is using her name and her business' name in fraud." He went on to explain the gist of the conversation with her attorney.

"Let's talk about what you've gathered so far about her situation and the questions you need me to ask her tomorrow."

Relief spread through Taylor like a wildfire in August.

Cleo was innocent, after all.

Chapter 7

The first thing that captured Rosebud's gaze in Albert's bedroom that night was the six-by-four foot mirror mounted on the ceiling above his bed.

Her second thought was how was he going to make use of it with his demanding mother always nearby? Mrs. Wilson certainly wasn't going to leave him enough free time to spend any with a woman.

Nordic Track equipment was under the window, which explained how he stayed in shape.

His mom's bedroom door had been closed all evening. She didn't offer Rosebud entrance or the tour of the apartment. The kitchen and living rooms were centered between the bedrooms, allowing each person a degree of privacy. They each had their own bathrooms.

The dinner Mrs. Wilson had prepared was superb with farm-raised catfish, jalapeño cornbread, seasoned collard greens and homemade potato salad. She'd even baked a pound cake from scratch served with fresh strawberries and cream. Rosebud couldn't remember the last time she'd had such simple, delicious southern fare.

Rosebud debated whether the dinner was worth the exhausting ordeal of the complaining woman's manipulation of the evening. It wouldn't do to expect Albert to walk her to her apartment. He couldn't leave his mom long enough to do so. Rosebud wondered how, with the woman's possessive nature, he could part from her long enough to work.

"Rosebud, I fixed up some leftovers for you to take home. Just warm it up tomorrow." Mrs. Wilson handed a paper bag to dear Rosebud.

Rosebud guessed that was her cue to leave and didn't hesitate to take it.

"Thank you for the delicious dinner. I'll certainly return the favor," Rosebud said, thinking that the more time she spent with Albert, Ronald was looking better and better. She headed for the door.

"You're welcome, dear." Mrs. Wilson smiled. "The arthritis bothered me so, but I got through it. Got to keep my Albert well fed. Women just don't cook the way they used to." She smiled up at Albert.

Rosebud looked at the woman's graceful hands that showed no signs of arthritis. It must be newly developed, she thought.

"It can be tough with a career." Rosebud guessed it was meant to be a cut at her since she served dessert from the gourmet bakery down the street.

"I'll walk you home," Albert offered taking the bag from Rosebud.

"Don't take long, dear. I need you to refill my prescription from the all-night CVS. I don't have many pills left."

"Okay mom. I won't be too long." Albert kissed her wrinkled cheek as if he were leaving for the week instead of a few minutes.

That trip to Greece was looking better and better to Rosebud. She was sick of Albert and his mom. Not even the opportunity for male companionship was worth this. He had no backbone.

"Don't bother, Albert," Rosebud said. "My apartment isn't far."

"Are you sure, dear? You know how dangerous it can be nowadays. I don't go anywhere without my Albert." She clutched his arm as though he'd fly away from her any moment. "Lord knows what can happen to an old woman alone." She shuddered, clutching her cane with the other hand.

If Albert tripped over his own foot on his way to her apartment, Rosebud knew the woman would never forgive her. She didn't want that on her conscience.

"I'm sure, good night."

"Hold on. I'll walk you on my way to the drugstore," Albert said.

"It's not necessary. . . ." Rosebud started. She only wanted to be alone.

"No problem." He patted his pocket. "I've got Mom's prescription in my pocket."

He held the door for Rosebud. After a parting smile and thank you to Mrs. Wilson, she left.

Silently, they walked to the elevator. Rosebud pushed the button. She looked at him and he smiled back at her. To look at him, one would never think that he was so spineless. Rosebud impatiently waited in the natural silence. She'd tell Albert tonight it wasn't working out.

The state-of-the-art doors swished open with barely a sound. Rosebud eagerly stepped in. They were alone in the elevator and he didn't even try to steal a kiss. She wondered again how he could let his mom control him so.

When they arrived at her door, Rosebud took her key out of her pocket and hurriedly opened it.

"Thanks for walking me," she said, and was about to shut the door when he stuck out a hand.

"You aren't gonna invite me in?"

Oh no, Rosebud thought, *I can't take any more of him tonight.* She sighed.

"Don't you have to get your mother's medicine?" she asked wanting him to leave immediately.

"I'll get it after I spend a few minutes with you. It's a relief to get away."

"You sure?"

"Yeah."

Resigned, Rosebud led the way into the room stopping by the radio to turn on her favorite jazz station.

He made himself comfortable on her couch. "I really do enjoy being with you."

"Yeah?" was all she could manage to say. She couldn't actually come out and say she couldn't tell by his actions. Rosebud sat on the other end of the sofa.

"It's nice getting away from Mom," he repeated. He slid to the edge of the sofa and took her hand. "She can be real demanding. But I'm all she has. She depends on me for everything. You understand don't you?"

Rosebud started to say she understood but settled on the truth.

"Actually, I don't understand. I don't want to criticize you or your mother, but you can help her without her clinging to you the way she does. It's not healthy for you or her."

"Dad died when I was young and she did everything for me. I owe her."

"I agree you should see that she's cared for, but not to the extent that you can't have a life of your own. She should have friends she can do things with like shop or play bingo or just to talk to.

"I realize I'm not the woman for you, but she won't allow one in your life and you cater to it."

"I'm trying to pull away, but it'll take time. Be patient, okay?"

Rosebud couldn't imagine herself that dependent on anyone. Cleo was her godchild and the closest she'd ever made it to motherhood, but she couldn't imagine imposing on her to that extent. Not that Cleo would let her.

"I just wish I could take you out more," he whispered softly.

"That's perfectly all right. Our relationship isn't that serious anyway." The whole conversation passed right by him.

"I'd like it to be more serious."

"I'm not ready for that. The man I dated for six years just left the area. I haven't decided whether I want to continue the relationship with him. I'm not ready for a serious entanglement with another man."

He sighed, casting his eyes downward, then looked up. "We can be friends, can't we?"

Rosebud smiled, "Sure." She did enjoy some of their conversations.

Albert groaned as he watched himself and the vision spread across him in the mirror above him, illuminated from the bedside lamp. He never made love without it.

Her long hair splashed over his hot skin, her hands doing unspeakable things to his body. Her hot tongue licked in his navel.

"What would the old biddy say?" she asked, her heated breath scorching his skin.

"Who cares," he groaned.

"But she needs her medicine," the siren whispered as she moved, her sharp nails seared a nipple, her tongue lapping at his thigh, cooling him, heating him.

"It can wait. I can't," he groaned and rocked his hips in readiness.

"But won't she hear us? You're very noisy." Her breath rushed over his skin.

"The old biddy sleeps like the dead," he assured her, pulling her up his body.

"If you say so," she purred. "I still don't understand why you put up with her demanding ways."

"She controls the purse strings. You know that, don't you?"

"And don't you forget it," she whispered. "We wouldn't want to become destitute. I love living well, and I love good, strong men."

His muscles tensed, knowing they turned her on. But not more than power—the power she held over him.

He'd played football in high school and he'd lifted weights since to keep himself toned. He had a whole setup in his bedroom just to keep himself in perfect shape for her.

Though he was fifty, not one ounce of flab showed on his hard frame.

She ran a hand down his arms and his chest ruffling the hairs.

Unable to stand the wait, he lifted her on top of him. He loved being on the bottom. He loved watching his hands along her hips in the mirror.

Most of all, he loved watching her head thrown back in the throes of climax.

Cleo had explained her entire life's story and more in the three hours she'd been in Gill Thacher's office. There absolutely wasn't one tidbit left to tell. She gingerly sipped on coffee.

Even now, the bag of mail stood beside his desk. He read the letters she'd opened two days ago and the letter she wrote to Mrs. Matherson.

He recorded the woman's phone number on his yellow pad. Cleo was sure he'd call Mrs. Matherson to confirm that Cleo actually talked to her.

She still didn't trust the attorney, but with a lawyer backing her up, she felt steadier. If it wasn't for the wrong being done to the senior citizens, she wouldn't be here now. She'd always worked for what she wanted. And she knew how hard senior citizens worked for every scrap they had. To have their life savings stolen from them was the worst of atrocities. For that, she'd gladly work with the U.S. Attorney's office. She straightened in her seat.

"Ms. Sharp, we'll look into this. Thank you for coming to us." He stood and shook her hand.

"Roland. How does next Saturday sound for a round of golf?" he asked.

"Seven okay?"

"Perfect. Give Pat my regards."

Roland escorted her out the office. The day suddenly looked brighter. And she'd probably sleep better for the first time in several nights.

"Now you can let them work on this case. If Gill needs anything, I'll contact you."

"That man is hopeless, absolutely hopeless," Rosebud said after she hung up the phone.

"What's wrong?" Cleo asked, as she listed the foods she'd serve during the open house.

"I don't know if I can stand to go out with Albert again. I know nothing serious will ever come of it." She put money in the cash register.

"What did he do?"

"His mother has too much control over him. I can't imagine the way he lets her stifle him. She almost pushed me out the door last night and wanted him to rush back afterward. I told him not to bother. I'd find my own way home." She paused as she broke a pack of pennies.

"We talked in my apartment. I kind of feel sorry for him. He's so nice and he'll never find a woman."

"You're still in love with Ronald."

"Ronald isn't here. At least Albert is a male to spend the time with."

"If the trouble is worth it. What about Ronald?"

"Unless he's ready to make a commitment, I'm not going to Greece. And when he comes back, I don't want to see him anymore. Even though, Lord knows, he's way beyond Albert. I'm not going to be his girlfriend forever. I'm not investing any more time in him if he's not as serious as I am."

"You've really changed, haven't you. Two years ago, marriage was the last thing on your mind," Cleo reminded her. "Ronald may need just a little more time."

"Too many failed relationships. Survival skills, I think. Now I need permanency. I want to know he cares as much for me as I do for him."

"I have a funny feeling he does. You've had plenty of phone calls and letters since he left. Ronald doesn't like to write, does he?"

The discreet bell over the door rang as Taylor entered. He wore his usual uniform of jeans and a T-shirt.

A fluttering sensation flowed through Cleo.

A football game wasn't exactly the theater and fine cuisine, but she'd enjoy being with him just as much.

Cleo thought that her position as employer might be responsible for his reticence about dating her. If the relationship went sour, he might feel his job prospects were threatened. That would be a financial disaster since he'd recently lost another job.

Tina, Ashand, and Bertrand arrived before Cleo had the opportunity to speak to Taylor.

"It's cold out there." Bertrand shivered.

"We're ready to go man." Ashand said.

"They're delivering the shelves this morning. Then we get to set them in and bolt them in place."

Cleo could barely hold her euphoria in check. Finally, she'd have the expanded shop she desperately wanted. More and more supplies were coming in every day to fill those shelves. She sighed happily.

"Just think, we won't be bumping into each other while we're packing supplies," she said to Rosebud.

"I can't believe you're not in there with them. You know you want to be."

"We went over the diagrams before. Taylor knows what to do," Cleo assured her. She had to almost sit on her hands to stop from going in there.

"Hmmp. You put a lot of trust in that man," Rosebud glanced at the closed door.

"If nothing else you can say he's an excellent carpenter," Cleo responded.

"I'll give him that, but that's all. Did that jasmine open his eyes?"

"If it did, he didn't show it. I wore my stirrup pants and he didn't indicate once that he was stirred. Maybe he isn't a leg man."

"Honey, if he's not a leg man, you've got plenty up top to tempt him." The dark roots were beginning to show in Rosebud's hair.

"We'll see Friday if I tempt him or not." Cleo was optimistic. She straightened up a few bottles that were out of place.

"We discovered another mailbox account with hundreds of letters. The owner hasn't been back in three weeks."

Taylor smothered a curse. "This happens over and over." He raked a hand over his head.

"But look at all these letters. Look at the money they're losing."

"Yeah. And they're still free to continue this routine. They aren't behind bars where they would be if they stayed one place long enough," Taylor said through gritted teeth. "They're always two steps ahead of us." It was Friday. Tonight he had a date with Cleo.

"Check the signatures and see if they match with the box in Germantown."

It was a brisk night. Taylor eased his arm around Cleo's shoulder to ward off the chill. Hundreds of people were packed into the stadium, from high school students to parents. This was a winning football team and they had the united support of the school.

Taylor watched the crowd around him. The atmosphere charged with tension and expectations with the rival school. Carter was No. 1 in the division last year, and Washington was number two. This year they were fighting neck and neck to win the title.

Taylor hadn't been to a game in so long that it took him back to his high school days.

Cleo rubbed her gloved hands together, puffs of vapor coming out when she spoke. Before he realized what he'd done, Taylor grasped her hands, rubbing them between his larger gloved ones.

He'd often watched her fingers mixing blends, displaying bottles as she demonstrated an item to a customer, tidying up. They weren't small, petite hands, but long graceful fingers. Taylor sucked in a breath remembering the many nights he'd dreamed of those hands stroking his body—all over.

His blood heated up even as the temperature sank more.

He was glad that, after winning the toss, Ashand started the kick-off.

By halftime they'd cheered so much Cleo was getting hoarse. The score was seven to three, Washington's lead accomplished by Bertrand blocking for Ashand to score.

The cheerleaders came out in their skimpy blue skirts and opaque tights, outfits not nearly warm enough to keep the blood flowing.

Taylor took a whiff of Cleo's perfume. Now that he knew she was innocent, his system found it difficult to remember that he was still working.

Best to put a little distance between them.

"Want a chili dog?" he asked her over the stomping and cheering.

Her warm lips opened, pulling his eyes. He leaned toward her and kissed her, just a little peck, but it shocked even him.

"I'll get that chili dog," he murmured. "Keep my seat warm."

"I'll do that," she whispered as if she'd be willing to keep something else warm, too.

Standing in the long line gave him time to cool his ardor. He made it back to his seat just in time.

They ate the chili dogs, sipped hot chocolate, and when a speck of mustard lingered on the side of Cleo's mouth, he found himself leaning forward to lick it off before he remembered and wiped it with a finger instead.

"Thanks," she said, took a napkin and wiped the spot again.

With the barrier of suspected fraud lifted, the desire he'd held in check went into overdrive. He wished he could tell her about the investigation. He wished he could do something to erase the worry from her face. Now, he could only wait until a future time.

She was exactly the kind of woman he liked. Self-assured, independent yet soft, strong yet yielding. A display of contrasts. He wondered why he couldn't have run across her sooner or in different circumstances.

Even now, Taylor realized he couldn't let his personal feelings interfere with his job. He wasn't looking forward to the volcano that would erupt when he told her his real occupation, that he'd been sent to investigate her.

Just for tonight, he'd enjoy a soft woman in his arms watching a high-school football game. He felt as free as a teenager snuggling up on the bleachers, munching on mustard and relish embellished chili dogs, and drinking hot chocolate.

Bertrand scored another touchdown. Taylor and Cleo jumped up and cheered. He forgot about work and the fact that he shouldn't be with Cleo.

Comfortably wrapped in his arms, Cleo glanced at Taylor. *Progress,* she thought. In miniature steps, but progress nevertheless.

Life couldn't be better. The six of them had worked long hours to get the shelves put up and now the shop was clean-looking and beautiful. A place any shopper would feel at home in.

Cleo counted her blessings.

She looked up at Taylor. His work was exemplary.

The fraud was in the U.S. Attorney's hands. Things were finally going in the right direction for Cleo.

Taylor and Cleo stood uncertainly at her door. Their attraction had sizzled all the way home. Forgotten was the game, but their closeness during the game was well remembered by both of them.

Taylor took the key and opened the door for her,

thinking he'd say good-bye on the doorstep. He didn't trust himself inside in her warm, inviting house.

"Well . . ." he started.

"Come on in," Cleo said.

"You've . . ."

"I could fix you a glass of wine to warm up," she offered in an inviting tone.

He'd fairly burn up with wine, Taylor thought.

"That may not be a good idea."

"I've never met a man so shy," she said.

"I'm not shy." Taylor stepped over the threshold not bothering to take off his coat.

"I'll take your coat."

He shucked the jacket handing it to her.

"Do you mind lighting the fire in the family room for me?"

"Not at all." Taylor was glad for something to do other than think of Cleo. Why should she have that effect on him dressed in her simple jeans and sweater?

He noticed the paper, kindling and logs were stacked. The room had started to cool.

After the fire caught Taylor put on four more logs and dusted off his hands.

What he didn't need was a blazing fire in a romantic setting and a seductive scent he didn't recognize filling the room.

"Ashand and Bertrand must be in heaven with their win," Cleo said, entering the room. "Oh, you got the fire going?" Her cheeks still glowed from the cold.

"Yes." Taylor sat on the couch and she joined him.

"I enjoyed that game."

"So did I."

"Did you really play basketball in high school?"

"Sure did, although I wanted to play football."

Her eyes raking him were like a hand stroking his most intimate parts.

"What position?"

"I wanted to be linebacker."

"Oh?"

"Do you attend their games often?"

She shook her head. "No time. Work takes up most of my time. Rosebud often reminds me I need to take time out for pleasure."

Taylor was sure she needed this time from work. She needed a man to make coming home a pleasure. Though Cleo's temperament would have her take pleasure from whatever she did, Taylor thought.

Facing each other on the couch, Taylor didn't want to leave, he wanted to be with her—wrap his arms around her. Taste her lips, enjoy her smile, touch her skin. Her eyes mesmerized him. She enthralled him.

Taylor reached out, ran a finger along her jaw. He captured her arm and pulled her close—his lips touching hers. He ran his tongue along the curve of her mouth, taking his time to savor her taste.

He'd just kiss her. That was all. But feeling her hand on his face enticed him to pull her closer. He entered her mouth, tasted her, ran his tongue along the roof of her mouth, then sucked on her tongue.

Taylor took his time to enjoy her, moving his hand under her sweater, caressing her skin. Skin that had enticed him for weeks—soft skin, sweet skin.

He shifted positions letting her head rest on his arm and shifted his hands to let them explore the soft curve of her breasts.

Unaware of who moaned, the sound gave him license to delight in her softness even more.

He opened the front clasp of her bra and touched the softness that spilled into his hands.

Cleo moaned, and her nail flicked his nipple. Taylor scooped her up and lifted her onto his lap, deepening the kiss, pressing her into him.

He leaned lower, grasped her nipple in his mouth, laved it with his hot tongue, knowing full well he couldn't take this to completion, but at the same time wanting to enjoy this for just a little while longer.

"Oh, Taylor," Cleo sighed.

His name on her lips were sweet music to his ears. He caressed her other nipple with his hand, testing the weight of her in his hands.

So soft, he thought. *Like silk.*

Cleo's finger touched his ear.

He leaned her against the couch, needing the feel of her under him for just a moment. Just a moment, he reasoned—he couldn't think at all, only feel.

"I've wanted to touch you forever."

She smiled up at him. "So have I."

With a low growl, he bent and kissed her swollen lips again. Her hands slid under his sweater sending hot tentacles of desire through him.

He stretched out against the length of her, rocking against her hips, loving the sensation he deepened the kiss. Releasing her lips, he slid down, looking at the beauty of her. Watching her eyes, he lowered his head and again captured a nipple in his mouth, sucking on it.

She moaned, her hand coming up to capture the

back of his head. He stroked the other nipple before leaning on his elbows.

"It's too soon for us." He didn't want to move. He wanted to stay where he was to complete what they started.

"I know," she whispered.

"I've wanted you for so long." He brushed the hair back from her face.

"I never knew."

"It was work. I didn't want to mix the two." He hated lying to her.

"That's what I thought." She ran a hand idly along his jaw. "What changed your mind?" she asked.

"You," Taylor whispered. "I couldn't wait any longer. But I'm still working for you."

"It doesn't matter."

It did, and Taylor knew it. He couldn't take her until he told her the truth, and he didn't have the authority to do so yet.

"Our time will come," he said.

Slowly, he sat up.

Eyes glazed, she peered up at him.

"We aren't ready to take this any further." He tugged her sweater down stealing a last touch.

Lying on the sofa was too inviting a pose. He pulled her up. "I've got to go, before it's too late to turn back." He stood and glanced at her again, pulling at his own sweater until it covered his heated chest.

He cherished that moment—wanting it indelibly etched in his memory. Her hair mussed, her features glazed, her lips swollen from his kisses, eyes dilated from need. From wanting him.

Chapter 8

Sunday afternoon was quiet but for the rattling of cellophane as Cleo and Rosebud filled gift baskets. The window display held pretty boxes and baskets also decorated with colorful cellophane wrap. They'd waved to several strollers who stopped by the window to admire the display.

Her quick fingers busily worked as Cleo thought of her evening with Taylor. He was thoughtful, insightful, and sensitive.

Still, it was best they took it slowly, giving them time to blossom before they became fully intimate.

Heat stole over her when she remembered their dalliance on the couch. If he hadn't stopped. . . .

He'd revealed more of himself Friday night than at any time since they'd met. There was a certain aloofness about him. A part of himself that he held back from everyone at the store.

Secrets, Cleo thought. She suddenly realized what bothered her about him. He reminded her of a man with secrets. One who couldn't afford to get too close to anyone, who held a portion of himself distant.

Perhaps it was better that way. At least until this ugly business cleared up.

On the other hand, a suspicious part of Cleo wondered what kind of secrets he harbored and why he had need of those secrets . . . if there were secrets.

Could his secrets have anything to do with her troubles? Then she remembered Rosebud's warnings. Cleo glanced at the woman out the corner of her eye. She couldn't erase the warnings from her mind.

Rosebud was still unaware of her problems. Cleo didn't want to worry her. Perhaps it was time she told her. Though Rosebud could be troublesome with her worrying and fretting, it would ease the burden by talking about it and her advice was often sound.

"Rosebud?" Cleo said.

"Yes?" she asked while she tucked cellophane in a gift basket with practiced fingers.

Cleo's hands continued working busily as she thought of a way to break the news.

"I've been having some problems lately."

"What kind of problems?" Rosebud stopped wrapping, giving Cleo her undivided attention.

"Someone's using my shop's name to sell fake cures," Cleo told her.

"What?" Baskets forgotten, Rosebud clutched a hand to her chest.

Cleo explained the events that had occurred to date. Rosebud was horrified.

"Girl, why didn't you tell me? Why'd you keep it to yourself?" Rosebud rose from the chair and came over to hug Cleo.

"I didn't want to worry you about it," Cleo said over her head.

Rosebud leaned back and grasped Cleo's chin in her hand. "What do you think friends are for?"

"Worrying." Cleo looked away from her and then back. "I've been thinking about Taylor and what you said about him," she divulged carefully.

"It's him." She demanded, immediately returning to her seat.

"Well, we can't be sure," Cleo cautioned her while setting her own basket down.

"I'm sure. I knew there was something about that man the minute I saw him." She pointed a finger. "You've got to fire him, Cleo, before he has you in jail."

"Let's not be hasty." Cleo cautioned again. "At least we can keep an eye on him here."

"Been around here all this time snooping. No telling what's missing." Rosebud glanced around as if she expected to find something missing right away.

"He hasn't done anything, really. It's just . . . he's so secretive. Everyone else in the shop is so open."

"Not him."

"Secrecy doesn't implicate him. Some people are introverts. They don't open up easily to strangers. And in his business, he's only there a short time. No reason to make friends," Cleo defended him unconsciously.

"Still," Rosebud said. "My vibes are telling me he's got something to do with it."

"Maybe I should casually mention it to Roland." Cleo ventured.

Rosebud nodded. "He could get that attorney fellow to look into it."

"I don't want to do that. We've no proof that he's guilty of anything and I don't want to get him into trouble. I'd feel better about following him myself."

"Let's do it." Rosebud's eyes brightened.

Cleo shook her head. "I was just thinking off the top of my head. We aren't detectives. What do we know about it?" Cleo's heartbeat quickened. It would be the thing to do. She had a lawyer now, but she still wanted to clear her name before the U.S. Attorney's office messed things up and these people got away or the attorney decided they needed a scapegoat.

With Rosebud hot on her heels, Cleo marched to the cabinet in her office. She pulled out the drawer.

"What are you going to do?"

"Look up his address." Cleo fingered through folders until she spotted his application and pulled it out.

"He's got a post office address," Cleo sighed. "That doesn't give us anything."

"Drat." Rosebud crossed her arms, tapping her arm with her fingers.

"Didn't he say he was coming by this afternoon to help out?" she asked.

"He did," Cleo said cautiously.

"We'll follow him when he leaves."

"I can't believe I'm going along with you," Cleo said, shaking her head in resignation. Rosebud was known to come up with some pretty adventuresome schemes in her younger days and had never outgrown them.

"Let's finish up everything before he gets here." Rosebud bustled back into the store.

Cleo shook her head and followed the woman.

She didn't like the idea of Taylor's involvement in illegal activities. Even now, the thought of him made her hot, and she could hardly believe he'd do that. He looked so clean-cut and honest.

It wouldn't hurt to check. At least this way she'd know for sure.

Cleo always felt better when she was proactive. Waiting for someone else to do the work for her left her with a great deal of unease. No one was more concerned about clearing up this scam than she. After all, she had her own best interests at heart, didn't she?

Cleo and Rosebud locked the store's door and hurried toward Cleo's car.

"Hurry up," Rosebud said, swinging her arm to motion Cleo on. "Or you'll never catch him." They ran to the car hoping Taylor didn't watch from his rearview window.

Cleo turned the ignition, backed out of her space and accelerated. He was already two stoplights ahead of them.

"Keep an eye on him. I've got to watch the traffic," she told Rosebud.

"I'm looking. I'm looking." Rosebud craned her neck. "But you've got to get closer."

The light turned yellow two cars in front of her. The first two cars made it through. As it turned red, Cleo accelerated, barely making it. The cars perpendicular to her blared their horns.

"Oh, shut up!" Rosebud shouted in her pique, forgetting to keep her eye on Taylor's car.

"Like they can hear you. I hope he doesn't spot us. Keep an eye on him."

"Hurry up. He's pulling ahead. He'll never recognize us in all this traffic." Excited from the adventure, she strained against the seat belt.

Cleo mashed on the accelerator, swerved into the passing lane, passed one car, charged back in the right lane to pass another, and swerved back in the left lane.

Car chases looked so easy on TV. It was hard in real life.

"You still see him?" she asked Rosebud, knowing they were crazy for attempting this.

"Barely. You're going to lose him. He's taking 295!" Leaning forward, craning her neck, Rosebud clung to the door handle with one hand and the dashboard with the other.

Cleo maneuvered two lanes over to the 295 exit and sighed. They stayed enough car lengths behind to keep him from noticing them.

"Rosebud?" Cleo started.

"Yeah?" Rosebud said, eagerness clouding her voice. She leaned back in her seat.

"I've developed a grave respect for private investigators," she said.

"Oh," she waved a hand. "It's exciting! I'm curious to see where he lives."

Cleo glanced at the older woman. "You and my mom must have been something together," she mused.

"That we were," Rosebud sighed wistfully. Then she perked up again.

"Looks like he's turning."

At the stoplight, Taylor looked in his rearview mirror and spotted a car that looked like Cleo's three vehicles behind him. Usually they stayed later than he at the shop. She also lived in the opposite direction.

The beep from a car horn prompted him to look ahead at the green light and accelerate.

He thought about his next move with Cleo. Boy she felt good in his arms Friday night. Womanly soft and sweet smelling. It took a great deal of willpower to leave her.

Soon, he hoped, he'd be in a position to pursue the relationship with her.

She didn't relax nearly as much as she needed to, with all the long hours she worked. He was just the man to look after her and make sure she did. She needed him, Taylor thought, as much as he needed her.

Even now he wished he could take her to his boat, sail out into the Potomac and let the water's sway relax her. She'd love his boat as much as he.

He usually enjoyed his own company on his boat, getting away to St. Michael's, Baltimore, or Annapolis or some secluded cove on the weekends.

But with Cleo with him, they could cast off early Friday and wake up Saturday morning to the music of seagulls and waves. It was still early enough to set off a few more times before the temperature dropped too much.

Hopefully they'd solve this case soon so he could get on with his personal life.

Parking his car at the marina, Taylor glanced in his rear-view mirror and noticed that car again.

Could she be spying on him? Of course not. He shrugged, smiled at his silliness, and turned off the ignition.

Walking to his boat, he turned up his collar. The wind had picked up. No sitting on the deck this evening to enjoy the water.

After a shower, Taylor zapped one of the dinners his mom had frozen for him and threw a salad together. Looking out the window, he noticed two women hovering together on the pier. It was too dark to identify them.

The women huddled together talking animatedly. Then they abruptly scurried out of sight.

Shaking his head, he took his meal out of the microwave.

The women, especially Rosebud, had acted peculiar all afternoon. But that wasn't strange, considering. Then he remembered the hostile look she gave him. For a time she'd begun to accept him. Also, Cleo had been unusually quiet. What could have happened between the time he left them at three and he returned at four?

Slowly, Taylor carried his food to the table. Sitting in the booth, he forked up the lasagna.

"It's him," Rosebud said.

"We don't know that," Cleo said. "We can't presume he's guilty simply because he lives on a boat. He could be visiting someone."

"He had a key."

"Still . . ." Cleo started.

"Listen, sister. There's no way an everyday working man can afford a boat like that. I went to some boat shows with Ronald and they cost a pretty penny. It must have been more than seventy feet."

"It wasn't that big, Rosebud. No more than fifty, anyway."

"Fifty or seventy. They still cost a fortune."

"Just a few hundred-thousand difference," Cleo said and slammed on her brakes when a car made an illegal turn in front of her.

"That's why I don't like driving in this area. People drive like they're crazy."

"They're just busy and always in a hurry. You would be too if you had a couple of kids and a full-time job." Cleo accelerated with the traffic. She grew wistful at the thought of children. Now and then she thought she'd wanted one or two. But what time would she have for them?

"What are we going to do next?" Rosebud asked.

"I've got to think about it."

"We need to keep an eye on him. Whenever he leaves, one of us needs to follow him." Rosebud grabbed the dashboard again as Cleo slammed on brakes. "Better you do it. I'd never be able to keep up with him."

Cleo didn't look forward to the idea. But with no other alternative, what else could she do? They had to know if he was perusing that box for mail orders.

"He's working in my house. He'll get suspicious if I fire him."

"I'll come over on the nights he'll be there. You can't trust yourself to be alone with him."

"I don't want to impose on you. I'll be fine. I don't think he'll try anything. He hasn't so far."

"I'm not about to leave you alone with him. I'll pack a bag tonight to move in until we solve this."

"Perhaps I should talk to Roland. I'm paying him to take care of my problems."

"Oh girl, please. What's he gonna do but tell you to wait for the authorities. No, we've gotta take care of this ourselves," she said firmly.

The fiasco nine years ago popped into Cleo's mind. "You're right. He'd be in the Bahamas before they realize what's going on." She left unsaid, *leaving her to hold the bag—again.*

Telling Rosebud about her troubles was the best thing she could have done, Cleo thought. Women were good at thinking problems through and getting things accomplished.

Still, sadness wrapped around her heart thinking Taylor would commit forgery in her name.

Chapter 9

Taylor glanced in his rearview mirror and spotted Cleo's car. So it had been Cleo and Rosebud at the marina. He smothered a curse. He was on the way to a meeting with Sam. He had to lose her—and fast.

His mouth turned up in a half smile, then he frowned. As amateurish as she was, she didn't realize yet how difficult it was to follow someone. Taylor looked ahead. He'd lose her at the intersection two blocks up without her even knowing he'd spotted her.

He whipped out of his lane, squeezing in front of an eighteen-wheeler and casually whipped back into his lane, then changed into the extreme left lane. Soon after, he noticed Cleo had squeezed in two cars behind his. A hundred yards from the intersection, he sailed to the right from lane to lane, making a sharp right at the intersection.

Taylor glanced up in time to see her pass by in the middle lane, unable to make the swift lane changes. He maneuvered several streets over, knowing she wouldn't find him when she circled back.

Safely on his way, he wondered at her following him. She suspected him of something. The question was, was it his role as spy or did she suspect him of mail fraud? Either way, it was time to tell her.

Even though Taylor knew he'd lost her, he made several more sharp turns and kept an eye on the rearview mirror as he drove to the office.

Once at the office, he met Sam and their supervisor, who had mixed feelings when they made the decision to tell Cleo his role as postal inspector. Better that than her having an accident or blowing his cover.

As soon as Cleo returned to the shop, Rosebud rushed over to her. "Where did he go?" she asked, excitement making her glow.

"I lost him." Cleo headed to her office, Rosebud on her heels. "I think he knew I was following him." Cleo shoved her purse in the drawer.

"You were supposed to stay a few cars back." She glared furiously at Cleo.

"I did." She dropped into a chair, annoyed at her own ineptness. Her thoughts warred between anger and disbelief. But Rosebud had caught him with some of her blends. Added to his guilty behavior, what else was she to believe? If he were innocent, he wouldn't need to play this cat-and-mouse game, would he?

"If he were going to another client as he said, he wouldn't need to lose me," Cleo stormed.

Cleo reflected on his good nature, his helpfulness, his kind disposition, and lamented the loss of it all. Why did he have to be a fraud?

Slowly, Taylor lifted a hand to ring Cleo's doorbell. He sighed, dreading the forthcoming task. Minutes ticked by while he waited for her. The car was in the driveway, indicating she was home.

She opened the door with a weary smile, using a towel to dab at the sweat on her skin. Her hair pinned up, he glimpsed ringlets of damp, curling hair on her neck. Taylor had to stop a moment as his heart skipped a beat. The form-fitting body suit she wore did nothing to calm his equilibrium.

He wanted to kiss her, but refrained from doing so.

"Hi." She stepped back offering a cautious smile he wondered at.

"Hi yourself." It amazed him how neat her place always was. Most people made a mess sometimes. She was probably one of those people who picked up after herself before dirt had a chance to root.

"I didn't realize you were going to work today."

"I'm not here concerning work."

"Oh?" Her eyebrows rose in question. He realized she was getting the wrong impression.

She indicated a chair in the family room where she'd started a fire in the fireplace. He sat on the overstuffed sofa leaning forward.

"Who's there Cleo?" Rosebud called out from somewhere down the hall.

"It's Taylor," she yelled back.

"Be right there."

"May I get you something to drink? I made raspberry tea," she offered.

"I'll have a cup. Thanks."

Taylor pulled his coat off, putting it on the arm of the chair. Standing before the comforting fire, he rubbed his hands together. His eyes followed her departing form, clearly outlined in the snug body suit.

When this was all over, he said to himself. He couldn't wait to get her on his boat.

Taylor let out a satisfied sigh. As soon as he told her his role, she'd be pleased he was looking out for her best interests. Actually—although he didn't like to mix business with pleasure—there was no reason they couldn't get things rolling right away. Taylor inhaled the scent of burning wood.

Rosebud entered wearing an eye-startling orange, red, and green caftan and smelling of roses.

She smelled fresh out of the shower. She also looked as suspicious as ever.

Cleo followed quickly on her heels, bearing a silver tray with porcelain pottery.

"I made a cup of tea for you Rosebud."

"I could certainly use one." She tapped a finger on the armchair.

Cleo sat the tray on the coffee table and poured a cup for Taylor first out of the teapot.

"I have sugar lumps and milk." She looked up at him. "What will you have?

"Two lumps of sugar, please."

Cleo spooned in the lumps and handed the cup and saucer to him. Before attending to her own and sliding back in an armchair to wait for whatever Taylor had to say, she fixed Rosebud's tea exactly like the woman preferred it.

Both women took delicate sips of tea and waited. Neither offered an opening.

"First, I'm not a carpenter by trade. I'm a postal inspector." He flashed a badge to show them. "I work for the government."

"So why did you hire on at my place?" Cleo asked, taking the badge to inspect.

"We suspected you of postal fraud," he said.

"That was low-down and dirty. Cleo never did a dishonest thing in her life." Glaring at him, righteous indignation had Rosebud slipping to the edge of her seat and shaking a fist at Taylor.

"Because of the health-food store I worked for in college?" Cleo asked.

"That didn't help. Actually, a few months ago we started to get complaints about Cleopatra's Aromatherapy's involvement in mail fraud."

"Why didn't you come to question me or charge me?" Her hand clamped around the chair was the only indication the news disturbed her.

"We were investigating you, remember? And we were aware of the incident you just mentioned."

"That . . ."

Cleo held a hand up to stop Rosebud's tirade.

"The company I worked for was involved. Not me. I was an innocent employee just like the other sales personnel." Her voice was strained.

This wasn't going as he'd planned.

"The owners were never found."

"I know that. Why are you telling me this now?" She asked bluntly.

"We've managed to subpoena some bank accounts and we discovered they weren't opened by you or Rosebud."

Her face tightened.

"You're here telling me this, so obviously there's a point to this."

She wasn't going to make this easy for him, Taylor realized.

"Yes. We need your help. I want to continue working for you undercover. We suspect it may be someone you know. Otherwise, why use your name or your company's name?"

"We don't want you to step foot in Cleopatra's Aromatherapy again!" Rosebud roared.

"None of my friends would do this to me. So you really won't have a purpose for being there."

"Has anything unusual happened lately?"

"You don't have to talk to him Cleo," Rosebud said and stood up.

"I presume you already know about the letters," Cleo continued.

"Probably been snooping all over the place," Rosebud snapped and began to pace. "Didn't I tell you I had bad vibes about him? Wasn't I right?"

"I told Gill Thacher everything. He can tell you everything. I suspect he already has."

"Why didn't you approach us sooner?" A shadow of annoyance crossed his face.

"You have the case file. Why do you think? The last time I went to you, I was blamed and fingerprinted when they couldn't find my employer. They thought everyone in the shop was involved and I was just covering my butt to stay out of trouble. What would you do under those circumstances?" Cleo stood. "Since this discussion isn't actually occurring at my business and you've finished your carpentry work, you get your tools and leave."

"That's right. I'll help you throw him out." Rosebud pounced.

This wasn't what he'd envisioned at all. "I need the inside track. I'll return the money you paid me."

"You did the job. You're entitled to be paid. Don't worry about the bathroom extension. I'll find someone else to do that."

"I'll finish the bath."

"I don't want you in my house, in my life, in my store. I don't want to see you again. Ever. You have access to my bank accounts, my post office box. Everything about my life." Cleo's voice rose with each sentence.

"I'm not the enemy here. I'm not stealing thousands of dollars from people who can't afford to pay it. And you aren't the one who has to go to an old lady's house and hear her tell you she's spent her last penny on a cure for her beloved brother! A cure that's no more effective than a piece of candy!" Taylor shouted.

"You people really amaze me. Where was your concern nine years ago when I came to you? I didn't see any helpful postal inspector then who was willing to work with me. No, he was ready to throw me in jail. Why should I trust you this time?" Her eyes clawed him like talons.

"Because I care! I want the people who're hurting these people, the people who're using your name. Your business integrity is on the line. If you don't care about them, think about that." He was rankled himself now with her callousness. If she didn't feel for their losses, then she'd at least care about her business.

"Another thing. This information stays with the three of us. No boyfriends, no close acquaintances. No one."

He leaned next to her, his eyes cold.

Rosebud got behind him and pushed. "Get out!"

He didn't bulge.

"The teenagers working for me are innocent," Cleo said as she glowered at him.

"That will come out during the investigation, won't it?" he snapped.

"Unlike you, I trust my friends."

"Then you have nothing to worry about. I'll work with your mail orders during the day and your bathroom in the evenings." How did it escalate to this, he wondered.

"I told you . . ."

"Somebody out there is using Cleopatra's Aromatherapy in an unfavorable light. Work with me or lose your business. It's that simple."

Which wasn't simple at all as far as Cleo was concerned. Cleopatra's Aromatherapy was her livelihood.

As he left, he heard "And don't you come here again!" from Rosebud. The door slammed. He'd wait until tomorrow to push the dating segment of his plan. He had to talk to her when Rosebud wasn't around.

From the family room window Cleo and Rosebud watched him walk to his car in long, easy strides. The first man who attracted her in years turned out to be a idiot! Humiliation sailed through her.

She'd been fool enough to let him kiss her—touch her—and she'd wanted more.

And he knew she wanted him while he was playing with her trying to soften her up for later.

No wonder Rosebud was down on men. She should have listened to those bad vibes from the very beginning.

Her healthy respect for Rosebud's vibes grew.

"Don't you worry." Rosebud hugged her and patted her on the back. "Everyone's entitled to mistakes."

"He worked in my store for weeks and I didn't know. I thought I was hiring a fellow small business owner." Cleo laughed a hollow laugh.

Rosebud led her to the sofa where the fire failed to warm her.

"Don't you let him undermine your trust. There are plenty of decent people out there, just like you. Look at those teenagers, for example. Any one of them will do anything for you, and you know why?" She put a hand to her heart. "Because your heart is pure."

Cleo smiled. Rosebud knew just the thing to lift her spirits. Only tonight it didn't work.

"And you'll find a man. One worthy of your trust. You mark my words. I've good vibes about that, too."

"Rosebud, this is such a mess."

"One you'll get over. You're surrounded by people who love you. I couldn't love you any more if you were my own child. It just tears me up that this is happening to you." Rosebud poured her a cup of restorative tea.

"I'll be okay." She gave Rosebud a tentative smile. "I love you, too, you know."

"I know you do, child."

"Tell you what, why don't we enjoy this nice fire I've made? Drink a glass of wine. I'll put on our favorite music and we can read our favorite books comfortably on the sofa. How does that sound?"

"Like pie in the sky."

On her way to the second bedroom she used as an office, Cleo passed the bath where Taylor had pulled the fixtures out. She couldn't stand the thought of having that hated, deceitful man working in her house.

And she couldn't do without her bathroom for very long. She'd have to get estimates from other carpenters. More time taken out of her schedule to interview them. Time she could ill-afford with the grand opening right around the corner. She massaged her temples.

She absolutely hated feeling helpless, and somebody out there was responsible for all this. She had no alternative but to assist Taylor in catching them. As much as she disliked him, the others were even more undesirable. She'd break the news to Rosebud tomorrow. Tonight, she and Rosebud would enjoy their books.

Cleo shivered, surprised to feel so cold. Then she realized she'd been exercising and her body suit was damp. She was almost finished anyway. She trooped to the basement to straighten up before peeling off the body suit to take a shower.

While soaping her body, she realized the scenes she'd dreamed of Taylor and herself would never be. His deceitfulness had botched all chances of a future with him.

Giving Cleo a chance to calm down, Taylor waited an extra day to approach her again. Determined to evade the spitfire, he arrived on Rosebud's day off.

Tina was manning the store, and Cleo was in her office staring at her computer screen.

She glanced up at his knock.

"I expected to see you yesterday," she said, forcing a cheerful facade.

"Thought you could use some time to recover." Taylor watched her weary glance.

"Consider me recovered."

If her smile could freeze, his nose would be frostbitten in seconds.

"I agree it's logical for you to continue working here. It'll give you an opportunity to observe anything unusual," she said stiffly.

"Even better if we pretended we were dating," Taylor broached the concept cautiously. "Then your friends will trust me."

If her lips tightened any more, they'd disappear, Taylor thought.

"That won't be necessary."

Taylor sighed. "Do we have to rehash this again?"

"Absolutely not."

"We made the perfect introduction at the game Friday night. No one would think it unusual."

"Give me time to soothe Rosebud. She won't like it and she can make it difficult for you working here."

"She's very protective of you."

"She's my godmother. What do you expect?"

"I wish this could have been handled differently, Cleo." He didn't know what else to say to her. He wouldn't apologize for his job.

"So do I, but there's nothing we can do about it now, is there?"

"I'll report to work tomorrow and resume the work on the Jacuzzi at your house."

Cleo watched him leave. Acclimating Rosebud to the idea of Taylor in the shop was tantamount to saying the Titanic was a little boat that sank.

At nine-thirty, half an hour before the store opened, Taylor entered Cleo's shop. Cleo's mouth tightened and she looked away from him. From the corner of her eye she watched him march in her direction. She squared her shoulders.

Henry was enjoying a cup of tea and a danish Rosebud had brought in.

"Good morning, Cleo," his breath whispered against her cheek just before he planted a soft kiss.

Cleo snatched away, giving him a stern glare, then looked at Rosebud whose keen eyes were glued disapprovingly to them.

Gearing up for a setback, he leaned closer and whispered, "Remember we're dating." He casually slipped an arm around her waist.

"Good morning," she said. They needed to talk and soon. This was taking acquiescence too far.

"How are you today, Rosebud?" he said, stretching the latitude given him.

"Fine," she responded tight-lipped, and unbending.

"I enjoyed myself last night," he whispered. "Did you?" he asked.

He looked at her as if he actually expected an answer. "Ah, ye . . . yes," Cleo stammered out.

"Good. I can't wait until tonight."

"Why," Cleo asked stupidly.

He shook his head and smiled. "Can I get you a cup of tea? What's today's flavor?"

"Ah . . ."

"Ginseng," Rosebud answered for her.

"Sounds interesting." He raised an eyebrow as he picked up a second cup.

"No, thanks."

He made small conversation with Rosebud and went into the back room to stuff baskets.

As soon as the door clicked closed, Henry said. "I didn't know you'd gotten a beau."

"He's just a friend." Her stomach roiled at lying to this nice man.

"Cleo?" Tina gushed. "I didn't know you were dating Taylor. He's to die for."

Cleo smiled. School was closed for teacher's work day and Tina asked for longer hours.

"So Ashand and Bertrand's matchmaking scheme worked," she offered, pleased.

"We'll see. We haven't sent out the wedding invitations," Cleo joked.

"Where does he live? He's so secretive."

"On a yacht at the Washington Marina."

"That's so romantic." Tina twirled around. "Living on a boat, sailing to the Bahamas. You'll be part of the rich and famous."

"I don't think so, Tina."

"You're so laid-back. My friends would just die for a man like him."

"Your friends are too young for a man like him."

"Cleo, you know what I mean."

Cleo tweaked the girl's braid. "I know exactly what you mean." Even after his deception, Cleo's heartbeat had accelerated when he kissed her. It must be—hell she didn't know anything anymore.

"Pulling anything out of you is like pulling water out of a turnip, my mom would say," Tina said.

"With the expansion, I haven't had time to think about it." She couldn't look at her friend and lie to her with a clear conscience. Cleo busied herself with setting out supplies. Tina returned to stocking shelves.

"Did you see Albert this weekend?" Cleo massaged her temples.

"He came over. That man is so boring."

"Write to Ronald." Being alone usually didn't bother Cleo. So why did the situation with Taylor strike her so? Probably because he reinforced negative thinking that it didn't do to trust.

"We'll see." They worked quietly for a few moments. "Do you know anything about Taylor's family?" Rosebud asked.

"No." Cleo glanced up.

"If you're supposedly dating the guy, don't you think you should know?" Rosebud said.

"It's pretend, not real."

"He works for you in your shop and your house. It's time you learned more about him."

Taylor walked back in with his cup.

Rosebud rolled her expressive eyes at Cleo.

Cleo turned back to her work.

"Were you raised in the area?" Rosebud asked him.

Cleo looked up between the two of them.

"No. I grew up in Atlanta."

"How'd you wind up here?"

"Work. I interviewed for this job while I was in college." He turned to Cleo. "Think we can get away after the lunch rush?" he asked her.

"No, I still run a business, remember." Her smile was brittle.

"Sure you can. Tina is here. You can get away." Taylor smiled encouragingly.

Cleo sighed.

"Will one-thirty be okay?" Taylor offered.

"Not for me! With everything I have to do I just can't take off in the middle of the day."

"You agreed, remember?"

Taylor ambled over to her. In what seemed an innocent gesture, he ran a hand around her neck and whispered, "If you keep this up, Tina will get suspicious."

Cleo glanced up to catch Tina watching them, a rapt expression on her face. "Check with me later," was the only concession she could give.

"I'll have to be satisfied with that," Taylor said. He took a sip of his tea, took her hand in his, kissed it gallantly, and left.

Tina laughed.

"He's laying it on a little thick," Rosebud said out the side of her mouth.

The man slicked a hand over his hair. "How long are we going to stay here. We've been here more than a year. It's time to move on," he said.

"Not too much longer. A month or two—no more than that." The woman put the finishing touch on her makeup. "There are so many different boxes to use here. That's what I love about cities."

"I know." He approached her and gave her a chaste kiss on her lips, knowing very well she didn't like having her lipstick smeared.

She leaned back and frowned. Turning back to the mirror, she applied more.

"We'll be able to retire after this tour and live off the proceeds the rest of our lives." Her voice was sultry, if not a tad irritated at him. Still that sultry voice always worked on him. They both knew that.

"I'm tired of moving from place to place. I'm ready to settle down. Make friends. Become a pillar in the community, you know."

"It will all come in due time. Trust me. You always have." She slid a soft hand along his cheek and left the bathroom that was much too small for her tastes. She was willing to put up with it to attain the greater reward.

"I'll see you tonight. You know the schedule."

"Yes, I know."

Chapter 10

Cleo sat in her office the next day eating her solitary sandwich. Taylor saw it as the opportunity to talk to her. Yesterday she was too busy.

With Rosebud assisting customers, for once he didn't have to worry about her interfering.

He observed Cleo, wishing he could say something, do something to break the impasse. Deeply involved in her paperwork, Cleo didn't detect his presence.

Dark smudges underlined her eyes. He was partly responsible for that, but not all. Why should he feel guilty for doing his job? He didn't commit the fraud, he simply tried to apprehend the people who did.

Taylor advanced into the office.

"Yes?" Cleo asked when he took the chair facing her desk. Her manner said he was the last person she wanted to see.

"We didn't get an opportunity to talk yesterday." He

said, scooting the chair back to accommodate his long legs.

"There are a few things I want to discuss with you." She closed the file so that only icons were displayed on the computer screen.

"Go ahead," he replied, regarding her tight, strained features.

"It's useless to appear intimate. After we've had a working relationship for so long, people would wonder at this sudden affection."

"Not really. We don't have months to develop this bogus relationship. We need to convince people immediately. Perhaps we could throw in that we've been holding back because of our working relationship in the store."

"I don't care what you're trying to convince them. Lay off it. The guilty party isn't connected to me."

Taylor merely shrugged his shoulders. "You can't flinch and move back every time I touch you."

"I'm not accustomed to your touch—don't need to become familiar with it—don't want to become familiar with your touch," she snapped.

"That's not quite true, is it?" Taylor stood and swiftly walked over to her.

Cleo scooted back in her chair and held a hand out to his chest when he sat on the edge of her desk, grasped her chin in his right hand as he leaned closer.

"No . . ." she shook her head, slapping his hand away and remembering when he kissed her before.

He leaned closer still until his lips touched her cheek. With his left hand, he stroked her neck, sending a featherlight touch over her delicate ear. He felt her shiver before she pushed him back and stood.

Taylor sighed and straightened. "I'm not so bad once you get to know me."

"Don't do that again," she gritted from between her teeth, edging away.

Taylor barely detected the slight tremor in her voice.

"I'm serious," he sighed, returning to the chair. "We need to appear as intimate friends, not enemies. Our date Friday night was a perfect beginning. We'll tell everyone that we fell for each other that night."

"Why do we need to say anything at all?"

"Tina, Ashand, and Bertrand will wonder."

"This is getting much too complicated. I don't see why you can't just subpoena the box, set someone on guard, and catch the guy when he arrives."

"It's not that easy. They change boxes every few weeks. By the time we find out about it, they've moved on."

"Don't they lose money that way? There must have been hundreds of thousands of dollars worth of checks in the bag I gave the U.S. Attorney."

"Sure, they do. They also evade getting caught."

"So what do you do in the meantime?"

"Wait for complaints, try to search out how they're getting these names."

"And in the meantime, I'm a sitting duck."

"With me guarding you."

"It would be more prudent if you worked on some tangible results of my case. For instance, I've gotten a couple of e-mail messages concerning these cures."

"May I see them?" Taylor asked.

Cleo handed him the two she'd printed out.

"Did you respond to them yet?"

"Yes. I checked my home page to make sure nothing

there indicated mail fraud. It didn't. So, I told them we didn't sell miracle cures and asked where they got the information. I'm waiting for their reply."

"Let me know when you get them."

"I will."

"Now back to the subject of what occurred after the game."

"Why? You used me."

"I didn't use you. I wanted you from the moment I met you."

Taylor showed up at Cleo's house with his tool belt, ready to work. The trick was to make sure she didn't shut the door in his face.

"I thought I told you not to come here again." She glared at him.

Taylor couldn't budge the locked screen door. "That's not an option."

She shut the front door.

"Wait, Cleo." Taylor banged on it and rang the bell.

"What do you want?" She opened the door again. "I agree that I have to put up with you at my shop. Not at home." Her arms were folded in an unforgiving manner.

"That's not reasonable and you know it. I need your cooperation if this is going to work. Your business is on the line. People's livelihoods are at stake, whether you like it or not. This is getting tiring."

"It sure is." She uncrossed her arms, unlocked the door, and sailed to the living room, indicating a chair.

He stood in the archway. "I'm here to work. I know you don't like this."

"You've got to be out of your mind."

"Cleo, it may be someone close to you. There's a reason they chose Cleopatra's Aromatherapy."

"Don't you think I know that?"

"Then work with me on this, not against me."

Cleo hated having anything to do with this man. But she wasn't a fool. After all, he wasn't the enemy.

That realization didn't keep the rancor at bay.

"I don't leave a job unfinished. What sense would it make for me to tear out your bathroom and not finish it?" he appealed to her.

She did need that bath finished. Making trips to the basement for a shower got old pretty quick. And she didn't have a tub at all anymore.

"All right."

"Have you had dinner?" she asked.

Surprised, Taylor said, "Not yet. I thought I'd work here a couple of hours then pick up something on my way home."

"Since you're fixing my bath for free, the least I can do is fix your dinner. Pork chops okay?"

"Sounds good to me." He sniffed the air. "Lavender?"

"Mixed with neroli and marjoram."

"Am I causing you that much stress?"

When Cleo looked at him surprised, he said. "I've been paying attention to your product."

Taylor watched her tight behind when she went to the kitchen. Reluctantly he turned to the bath. Tonight he'd pull up the floor.

* * *

Cleo's original plan was a sweet potato with a salad for dinner. That wouldn't do for Taylor. Padding to the freezer, she pulled out pork chops and soaked them in cool water. Letting them thaw, she washed two sweet potatoes and stuck them into the oven. After mixing a salad, she tested the pork chops and discovered they'd thawed enough to bake.

She listened to him rip up tile and decided music was in order. She started to put on Luther, then realized he'd be too romantic. Led Zeppelin would be much better.

Heat stole over her remembering what occurred after the game. Cleo poured a glass of wine to sip as she cooked and then set the table. She opted for the dining room over the kitchen.

In an hour Cleo called Taylor to dinner.

Passing through the kitchen, Taylor noticed potted herbs growing on the windowsill. He couldn't identify one from the other, but wasn't surprised that she grew her own. She clipped a sprig of something and chopped it up into the salad.

The candlelight and flowers on the table surprised him. "All this for me?" he asked.

Cleo declined an answer.

"I'm surprised Rosebud isn't here tonight," Taylor mused as he forked up salad.

"She only came because she thought I needed protection from you."

"Protection from me?" he repeated. "Why?"

"We thought you were the one framing me."

"I wonder where you got that notion?"

"Rosebud suspected you from the beginning because of your snooping, really. And there were those bad vibes.'' The steam rose from the baked pork chops with apples and raisins.

"I'm just an everyday, clean-cut, honest guy.'' Taylor's stomach all but growled at the tempting fare.

"That's what I told her. I was wrong. You only look innocent.''

"Everything all set for the open house?''

"Yes.''

"I'll work it with you.''

"Most of the work comes before and after.''

"What can I do to help?''

"Nothing, really. I just don't . . .''

"Don't tell me you don't trust me because you know it's not true. You're just angry with me. You may as well put me to work since I'll be hanging around anyway.''

Cleo had to concede that he'd look conspicuous if she didn't put him to work.

"Think of all the free labor you'll get.''

"You'd be better off thinking of who's setting me up.''

"We've got a whole team working on that. They won't get away this time.'' He wanted to reach over and gather her hand in his. He couldn't yet. And he wondered how long it would take her to thaw.

"Well, we better eat before the food gets cold,'' she said.

Taylor paused. "Cleo, we need to talk about what happened Friday night after the game.''

"What's to say? You used me.''

"That's not true. I wanted you the moment I saw you. But I couldn't do anything about it because of my position.''

"We don't have to go into this.''

"I think we need to."

"It's over and done with."

"I still want you."

"Well, you can just forget it."

"You're not being honest with yourself or me. Now, there are too many hostile feelings, but I hope soon we can put my job behind us and approach this like two people who are attracted to each other."

"I don't think I can ever trust you again."

Taylor's fingers tightened around the fork. "I hope you don't mean that because you're the first woman I've been attracted to in more than a year."

Taylor picked up his fork and bit into the crisp salad coated with fresh blue-cheese dressing.

The meals he fixed himself on the boat were quick affairs. Taylor sighed. It looked as though he wouldn't get her on the boat anytime soon.

Taylor arrived almost nightly to work on the bath and Cleo fell into the routine of preparing dinner or bringing takeout. Some evenings Taylor would call telling her not to cook, that he'd picked up pizza or Chinese.

He was slowly worming his way into her heart again, Cleo thought. She wondered if he had ever left. Perhaps her feelings were merely sidetracked when she'd discovered his true identity. It still rankled that after working with her, he believed she could have defrauded people.

It was a surprise when he asked her out to the Clamor Club one Saturday night.

"I don't think so," Cleo responded.

"Come on. When was the last time you went out for fun?" he asked engagingly.

Cleo smiled. "Okay, I can't remember."

"Be ready in an hour."

Cleo wore a long-sleeve emerald-green dress with a scooped neck. With it, she wore a gold necklace, earrings, anklet, and black, comfortable two-inch heels perfect for dancing. Surprised, she looked forward to going out.

Taylor wore gray slacks with a sports jacket and casual shirt.

They arrived around nine and sat at a table in a quiet area. Taylor scooted his chair to sit next to Cleo, giving him a view of the dance floor.

A waitress immediately came over. "What can I get you folks?" she asked.

"What would you like, Cleo?"

"Strawberry daiquiri."

"I'll take white wine," Taylor said.

As soon as the waitress left, the deejay started a slow number. Taylor didn't miss the opportunity to hold Cleo in his arms.

He tucked a hand in the small of her back as they walked to the dance floor, the lights low and intimate. They carved out a spot on the crowded floor.

"It seems I've waited forever to get you in my arms again," he whispered as they moved slowly to the beat.

Cleo glanced up at him enjoying the feel of his body pressed against hers.

"It's been a while. Two weeks ago, I would have thought we'd never get to this point."

"I'm glad we're here."

"So am I."

He tightened his arms around her letting the slow beat cocoon them, wrapping them closer and closer.

When the song ended, they returned to their table, Taylor putting his arm around the back of Cleo's chair. The waitress soon arrived with their drinks and Taylor paid her.

Cleo sipped her daiquiri. It was perfect.

"So, Ms. Sharp. Did you dream of being an aroma-therapist as a child?"

"Oh, no. I dreamed I'd be a singer, just like millions of little girls. I was going to be the female version of Michael Jackson. He was every child's idol, I think. And you?"

"Um. I was going to be a teacher. Then I could marry Ms. Graham, my fourth-grade science teacher."

"And what would you have taught?"

"English. Then I could read sonnets to my true love."

"And did you ever read sonnets to your love?" She smiled at the image.

"I lost all interest when Harriet found the one poem I created and laughed at it."

"Ouch."

"Not good for the ego."

Taylor observed her as he listened to the music. She'd relaxed enough to let her guard down.

Dark circles still outlined her eyes. She needed to rest. Come hell or high water, as soon as the open house was done, he was getting her on his boat to sail on the Chesapeake.

Taylor cleared his throat. "Perhaps next weekend we can go out on my boat. I haven't had time to take it out lately. Since the open house is Friday night, you should be free. You can get one day off, can't you?"

"That's pushing it."

He touched the delicate skin under her eye. "Lady, you've got bags here. You need to get away more than I do. Besides, I want some uninterrupted time to give us a chance to get to know each other."

"Taylor, we aren't ready for this."

"The attraction's there for both of us. I'm not asking for sex. Just a couple of days with you. You'll have your own space. We'll be tourists."

Any sane person would have hired a caterer to prepare the food for the open house. Not Cleo and Rosebud. Under Rosebud's directive that you didn't need to spend the extra money to have somebody cut up oranges and watermelon, they worked in the kitchen Thursday, the night before the open house.

They'd washed and dried dozens of oranges, and now, Cleo, with sharp knife clicking rhythmically against the cutting board, sat at the table slicing oranges while Rosebud carved a hothouse watermelon rind in an intricate design.

Cleo thought Rosebud devised projects for moments like this when the place was quiet and they talked. It was the perfect opportunity to discuss Taylor.

"Rosebud?"

"Yes?" She wielded the cutter expertly, never glancing away.

"We need to talk about Taylor."

Her hand stilled.

"That traitor. Why?"

"I don't see him as quite the villain anymore."

Rosebud inhaled sharply. "Don't you let your hormones rule your head."

"It's not that." Cleo sliced an orange in half.

"What is it then?" she asked as she resumed her carving.

"The people who sent the mail out using Cleopatra's Aromatherapy are the villains. They're the ones hurting me. I've been thinking about it a lot."

"And?"

"This doesn't end when they catch these people. Thousands of people know the name Cleopatra's Aromatherapy in an unfavorable light. I'm going to have to rebuild my business' name or I'm going to have to change names."

Rosebud had stopped carving again. "You're right. I didn't think of that."

"They've stolen my identity. At least Cleopatra's Aromatherapy's identity."

"Oh Cleo."

"So what Taylor has done is nothing in comparison."

"Maybe he has some ideas."

"I haven't broached the subject with him yet. I've been too angry—at the wrong person—to consider all the implications of this situation." She sighed. Nights when she only slept two hours. The seven-day weeks she'd put into this. And where did it all end?

"I'm just as guilty."

"We were thinking emotionally. We've been busy the last month preparing for the expansion and tomorrow night's grand opening. We're frazzled."

"Girl you need time away from here."

"I can't take time away."

"Yes, you can. The shop's not going to disappear just

because you take a few days off. You haven't been away more than ten days in three years. And you haven't taken two days off since you moved into that house."

"You work just as hard."

"I had three vacations last year. How many have you had?" Rosebud gazed at Cleo, her stare unwavering.

Silence hovered in the air. Finally Cleo said, "Taylor wants me to go away with him on the boat for the weekend."

"You like him, don't you."

Cleo nodded slowly. "Yes, I do. Isn't that crazy? I like a man who doesn't trust me."

Rosebud smiled, a sadness shadowing in her eyes. "It's not crazy at all. I know that if I was one of those people who'd lost all that money, I'd want a Taylor looking out for my interests."

"I guess they get all the grief, but not the glory."

"So, when are you going to tell him you'll spend the weekend with him?"

"I don't know that I am. I don't have to spend it with him. I can just take a few days and visit the museums, shop, or go to the movies. Gosh, I don't know the last movie I've seen. I can take in a play. There's plenty I can do right here."

"If you're here, you'll think of an excuse to come in to work. I know you, Cleo," Rosebud said, her manner serious.

"I'll try very hard not to."

A shrewd look appeared in Rosebud's eyes.

Chapter 11

The workroom where Taylor had arranged tables the night before did for aromatherapy what a palatable arrangement of food did for a restaurateur. Ashand, Bertrand, and he had lifted and rearranged tables and sanded and stained the "new" tables Cleo had purchased. They now held center stage.

When Cleo and Rosebud had literally pushed Taylor out the door last night around midnight, the women had just begun to cover the tables with pressed white tablecloths. Now, each table featured a different arrangement of gift baskets.

Some tables displayed products centered around a huge natural sponge. Satin pillows, eye pillows, essential oils, lotions, and decorated tall glass bottles filled with bath salts and perfumes, tempted the eye.

Tables held pastries, punch and tea, orange slices, cheese balls, chips and dip, nuts, and the carved melon holding different fruits with watermelon balls. Since Taylor missed dinner, the food especially appealed to his senses.

People wandered from the shop where Rosebud and Tina were holding court to the converted packing room where Cleo and Ashand stood guard, mingling among the guests. A woman Taylor had yet to meet refreshed the food trays.

Tonight an orange citrus scent spilled into the air from the aromatherapy fan.

The most beautiful sight of all was Cleo decked out in an off-white suit and a red blouse accented with pearls. The hem of her skirt hit two inches above her knee. Taylor glimpsed more than one male eye regarding her. He wanted to shout that she was all his.

The contrast between the winter-white skirt, her skin, and the red was particularly striking.

His eyes left her legs and wandered slowly upward. He found her regarding him. She looked away from him, not even hinting at the smile he longed to see.

Since their conversation, she'd begun to thaw a little toward him. She had even agreed to the boat trip.

Taylor decided to take two days of leave, thus giving them four days together. To say he was eagerly awaiting her arrival on his boat was an understatement. Rosebud had become his companion in strategies for getting Cleo away.

He'd listened to the weather for tomorrow before coming over. They predicted temperatures in the eighties. Perfect for boating. He hoped they'd soon come to some sort of truce.

Cleo glanced up as Taylor poured a cup of punch. He was devastating in a sports jacket and slacks. Cleo wondered if he had to get them specially made.

Though he'd called an informal truce, she was still nervous about spending four days in the confined quarters of a boat. The two of them sharing a bathroom and kitchen, bumping into each other at every turn. And she couldn't just hop up and leave at will.

No strings attached, he'd said. Two friends on a platonic mini-vacation. Cleo gazed at him as he conversed with one of her customers and knew she was crazy for even considering going away with a man she scarcely knew.

The episode after the game still flashed in Cleo's mind. The kiss wasn't platonic. The weight of his body stretched out on hers certainly wasn't platonic. And the caress of his hands over her heated flesh wasn't platonic. That and his hands were lethal. She enjoyed the feel of him much too much and even craved more.

Heat flashed over her skin when she caught him looking directly at her. At that moment she had two reasons for cheer—he couldn't read her mind, and her complexion didn't turn red with embarrassment.

Cleo tried to remember that he was just doing his job.

Unfortunately, she caught herself gazing at him when her thoughts should be elsewhere. It would be prudent to maintain some distance, especially with them staying in close quarters for the next few days.

She caught Clark Bryce advancing on her. "Hello Cleo."

"Clark," Cleo answered. He and his wife, Barbara, owned a chain of hair salons in Virginia and Maryland, where the African-American population had grown but didn't have hair salons to fill their needs. There were four in Prince George's County alone, not to mention Fairfax and Montgomery.

The looks of him alone was enough to bring the women. He was so cute that, if he weren't married, one might think he was gay.

"I'm happy you could make it tonight. How is Barbara?"

"Good. She's working tonight and hated missing this. We'd like to carry your products in our shops."

"The test market went well, I trust?" Four months ago, Clark had tested some of her products in one of his shops.

"Better than I expected. I'd like to carry a regular supply of the high-sale items." He handed Cleo an order form. "I've listed the products I want. I was wondering if you could set up a display in the shops. Obviously, you know how best to show your things."

"Of course. Let's set a time when we can get together to talk about the display and a time frame."

"Good. It's always good to see you, Cleo." He looked at his watch.

"Tell Barbara I said hello."

"Will do. She'll invite you to dinner soon."

As Clark walked away, Cleo glimpsed Taylor. He frowned as his gaze followed Clark and sauntered in Cleo's direction.

"We'll be closing in a few minutes," she told him.

Cleo went to greet the last two people on their way out the door.

"You've got nothing to complain about tonight," Taylor said when she returned.

"I'm pleased," she said, grabbing a tray of food. "The evening went well. More companies sent representatives than I even expected. From hotels, beauty salons, both large companies and small."

Taylor grabbed another tray, stacked it with the teapot, cups, and saucers and carried them to the kitchen.

"Did you pick up promises or actual contracts?"

"Both," she said as she prepared to fill the dishwasher with cups, saucers, and dessert plates.

Taylor pulled off his jacket and rolled up his shirt

sleeves. In an unspoken agreement he rinsed off the dishes and she stacked the dishwasher.

"Did you know any of them well?" he asked, handing her a plate.

"Some." She looked up, the plate in her hand forgotten. "Why?"

Taylor took the silverware and scrubbed it with the brush.

"Do you think any of them could be responsible for the fraud?"

"Absolutely not. No reason for it." She shook her head. "They all have successful businesses."

"We have to look at every angle, that's all." He leaned over and put the silverware in the holder while Cleo wiped the table.

"You can't be suspicious of everybody."

"It's my nature."

They went back into the converted packing room to get the last of the dishes and wipe down the tables, then joined Rosebud and the teenagers in the shop.

"Thanks guys for a fruitful night."

"I'm so tired, I could drop," Tina said. "But I enjoyed it." She clutched her chest. "I can't wait until we have our own store."

Ashand groaned and rolled his eyes. "Here she goes again."

"When I go to your open house and you're floating on a cloud, I'll remind you of this moment," Cleo said to him playfully.

"Why don't you young folks go. We're all cleaned up in here."

"Night everybody," they called out.

Rosebud grabbed her jacket and admonished Cleo to enjoy her vacation.

"I really shouldn't take so much time away."

"Don't you dare." Rosebud ushered her out the door and locked it. "I don't want to see you until Wednesday morning." She looked to Taylor. "See to it."

"Yes ma'am," he said smartly."

" 'Bye, kids."

"Cleo, why don't I follow you home. You can stay aboard tonight and we'll cast off first thing tomorrow morning. That way you won't have to get up so early." He braced himself for an argument.

"All right." She turned and went to her car without further comment.

It was a moment before Taylor forced himself to move. She must be more fatigued than he realized. But Taylor didn't tempt fate by offering a comment.

The short drive to her house was accomplished in ten minutes.

"My luggage is already packed," she said once they were inside. "Do you mind if I take a shower and change before we leave?"

"No. A Motown Special is coming on tonight. If you don't mind, I'll watch it."

"Sure. I want to record that. I'll stick a tape in."

They went to the family room where she rooted around for a tape. Flipping on the television, she set the timer and station on the VCR then disappeared into her bedroom, pulling out jeans and a shirt to wear to his boat, and wondering if she'd packed the proper clothing for the trip.

Chapter 12

The temperature had dropped and the wind had picked up on the water. Taylor's yacht rocked softly in the darkness. Pinpoints of lights shone from what looked to be hundreds of boats—power boats, sailboats, and houseboats—at the Washington Marina.

Cleo had envisioned something much smaller than what she actually glimpsed. She looked up to the helm and scanned down to the black water rushing below. This was a luxury yacht.

Taylor took Cleo's arm as they walked down the dock to his boat. Located on the end, it barely shifted as they boarded.

Protected in the enclosed deck, the wind seemed far away while Cleo waited for Taylor to unlock the cabin door. As soon as he entered, he flipped on the light.

Cleo didn't know what she expected as she crossed the threshold since she'd never been on a yacht before, but it wasn't the blue and white plush interior before her, or the comfortable-looking blue leather L-shaped couch.

"Have you been aboard a yacht before?" Taylor asked, looking like the trials of the day immediately washed off him.

Cleo shook her head.

"We're in the salon," he said as he closed the door. The cherry wood gleamed in the neat room. It also boasted a complete entertainment system with a TV, VCR, and CD player. The only thing out of place was a *Washington Post* left on the ottoman.

"Down the steps in back of you is the aft master stateroom." Taylor continued his travelogue easing her bag to the floor and pulling off his jacket.

Taylor took the paper bag Cleo carried and she trod to the door to take a look. A queen-size bed covered with a blue and white print spread took up most of the room, with just enough room left for a tiny aisle on each side. Limited storage cabinets were on each side and underneath the bed.

She was glad she'd packed light.

"How long have you lived here?" she asked as Taylor approached her.

"Six months."

Taylor picked up her suitcase as they continued to walk slowly through the cabin.

"Straight ahead is the galley and dining room."

Cleo paused to look at the U-shaped space with faux granite fiberglass countertops. The stove had three burners. A microwave and a coffeepot completed the picture. Taylor had set the grocery bag on the counter.

All the comforts of home, Cleo thought as she glanced down to see a small refrigerator/freezer stored under the counter. She liked the dining room most of all with its bank of windows overhead. She looked forward to seeing the view in the morning. Everywhere else, window space was scarce.

"To the left is the laundry room," Taylor pointed out as they advanced. "I had a choice of making this into another stateroom or full laundry room. Since I live on board, I settled on laundry."

Cleo looked at the countertops, cabinets, and front-loading washer. "Where's the dryer?"

"It's a washer-dryer all-in-one."

"Everything you need."

"And more," he replied before urging her on.

"In front of you is the forward stateroom where you'll sleep. Unless you want to join me," he half joked as he put her suitcase on the bed, then stepped back to lean against the bulkhead.

"The forward stateroom will do nicely, thank you." And it would, Cleo thought as she perused the full-size pedestal bed with its striped dark and light blue spread.

"Through that door is your head with full shower."

Cleo didn't know she was holding her breath, pleased that she'd be at the other end of the yacht and wouldn't have to share a bath with him. Visions of bumping into him on her way out of the shower with only a robe to cover her and leaving the scent of her soap behind was just too intimate. Then her eyes settled on Taylor.

He looked tired, she thought. Having to do three jobs wore on him. After working hard all day in her shop, he went to the postal inspector's office. Most evenings, he'd work on her bathroom. And never complained to her about having to do both of them.

For the first time since she discovered his true identity, she wanted to walk up to him and hold him.

A dangerous thought.

"Well, it's late. I'm going to shower and get ready for bed. You know where I am if you need anything." Like a predator he advanced on her. "Most of all, this is your home for the next few days. Welcome aboard, Ms. Cleopatra Sharp." He kissed her lightly, turned and left before she could respond.

A kiss shouldn't have left Cleo's stomach jumping. It was designed to be a simple touch. She just sat on the edge of the bed gulping in a deep breath, carrying a hand to her lips.

Getting through this weekend would prove interesting, Cleo thought. Taylor left her with warring emotions of hesitance and eagerness. This behavior was uncustomary for her. She never hesitated to take the lead if she wanted something, but with Taylor . . . she'd leave the whys for later. Cleo rose to unpack and store the food she'd bought and then unpacked her suitcase, making use of the drawers.

The boat rumbled to life as Cleo came out of her stateroom, unable to believe that she'd slept so late.

A quick glimpse out the window promised a bright, clear day.

Wearing jeans and a T-shirt, Taylor entered the cabin whistling cheerfully. He stopped and gave her a wolf whistle. "I like you in jeans," he said. "Cast off in five minutes, okay?" he asked casually.

"All right." Finally they'd be on their way. It still wasn't too late to turn back, Cleo thought and knew she wouldn't dare. The spirit of the trip pumped her adrenaline.

"We'll stop in Old Town for breakfast and Pope's Creek for lunch, if you like crab legs as much as I do."

"I love them, but I can put something together for breakfast."

"All right," he smiled. "Come on out to take in the view. I'll put the top back so we can get the crisp morning breeze."

Cleo grabbed a windbreaker from her stateroom and followed him out, climbing the high stairs to the helm.

She got her first glimpse of the marina in daylight.

A tiny breeze stirred the water—rippling and inviting. It was cool in the early morning, but Cleo found it refreshing.

She saw a few boats leaving their slips as she got her first glimpse of the helm's instrument panel and wondered at how difficult it would be to monitor them. Driving a car seemed much easier in comparison.

Two comfortable-looking captain's chairs and a lounger offered seating on the helm. If she blocked out the houseboats, looking down on the water felt like looking down on the world.

"What can I do to help?" she asked Taylor.

When he fixed those gorgeous eyes at her, she couldn't move.

"You can cast off the bow and stern lines. The bow lines are in front on either side of the boat and the stern lines in back. Just unloop them from the cleat and leave them on the finger pier."

Cleo looked down the side. "I can walk on that?" she asked skeptically.

"There's plenty of room around there and a handrail to hold on to."

Cleo looked at him askance as he tinkered with the dials. She descended the stairs and eased along the narrow aisle. From this point she was very close to the water and no longer felt on top of the world. She made it to the bow thinking Taylor and she differed vastly on this point because they certainly had different views of "plenty of walking room."

When Cleo looked toward the helm, she saw that he'd

taken the top off. "Do you want me to leave the rope here?"

"Yes," he called down. "We have more on board."

Cleo made it around and untied the other rope before she maneuvered herself to the rear to release the stern lines.

"All done," she called up from the deck.

Taylor had put on his windbreaker and the wind ruffled it as he leaned over.

"Ready to cast off? Come on up and join me."

"Let me get the coffee and pastry first. I don't want to miss a thing," she responded excitedly.

Cleo quickly disappeared into the cabin and stuck croissants stuffed with cheese into the microwave and poured the coffee as she waited for the food to heat.

She put the sandwiches in napkins and carried them with the coffee up to the helm.

"Thank you," Taylor said as he took the coffee and put it in the cup holder.

Cleo sat in the captain's chair beside Taylor. The wind ruffled her hair.

Taylor put the boat in gear, gave it throttle, and pulled away.

"We're in the Washington Channel now," he said after a few minutes.

"Isn't that Ft. McNair?" Cleo pointed to the left.

He nodded, "And we're coming up on Hain's Point on the right," he pointed out.

Cleo had a grand view of "The Awakening" and soon National Airport's planes ascending and descending in rapid succession.

She glanced at Taylor. The worry lines erased from his face, a sense of anticipation oozing from him.

She noticed the wind picking up as the boat gained speed past the Point.

"Ready to eat?" she asked him and he nodded in response. She handed him a sandwich and bit into her own, not taking her eyes from the view for even a moment. The Potomac surrounded them with only a sprinkling of boats out.

When Taylor finished, Cleo handed him a napkin and took a sip of coffee that tasted perfect on the cool morning. She usually preferred tea, but somehow coffee seemed more fitting.

After passing Dangerfield Island, Old Town, Alexandria, came into view. People were walking around, getting an early start on their day.

"Wanna stop?" Taylor asked.

"Yes," Cleo said, realizing it had been years since she'd last visited. They pulled up to the pilings at the dock along with the other boats at the waterfront.

They strolled the streets for an hour, stopping by Bread and Chocolate for more pastries before they headed off again.

On the left, bass fishermen fished in the little creek along the hydrilla. They passed under the Woodrow Wilson Bridge. Ft. Hunt and Jone's Point were on the right. People biking down the path along the river waved at them.

At one point Cleo went to the cooler in the helm for sodas.

By the time they reached Pope's Creek, Cleo was almost famished. She got out again to hook the stern lines.

When she came back aboard, Taylor grasped her hands. "Look, let's make a pact. We won't think or talk about work until we get back okay? I've enjoyed this morning with you.''

"I feel ten years younger. Thank you for suggesting this trip,'' she said.

"Captain Billy's sells the best crab you've ever tasted. Let's enjoy, okay?''

They dined and walked around, returning to the boat to finish their journey to Solomons Island. It was late when they arrived and they were both exhausted—happily tired. They got a dock hookup where they connected to electricity, water, and even cable which was a rare treat while Cleo put together a light dinner.

Taylor showered first, with Cleo waiting until after dinner to shower. That evening, they relaxed in the salon, their feet resting on the ottoman.

Taylor took her hand in his. "It's been a long day, hasn't it?''

"It must have been a tiring one for you. I only had to ride and enjoy the view.''

"I enjoyed it. Believe me.'' It was Saturday night and they waited for *The Josephine Baker Story* to air on cable.

"I want to get to know you, Cleopatra Sharp. What makes you tick, what makes you happy? Your wildest dreams and what makes you sad,'' Taylor said suddenly.

"I don't know if I like the idea of you knowing everything about me. A woman has to keep some sense of mysticism about her.''

He gave that crooked smile Cleo liked so much. "I want to know all your deepest secrets.''

"Believe it or not, I'm like an open book. You already know my life's history.''

"Not true. I don't know the first man you ever fell in love with.''

"That's easy. His name was Mr. Stonner, my Sunday school teacher. I was six at the time."

They laughed.

"Who was your first love?" Cleo asked.

"My kindergarten teacher." They laughed again at the silliness.

"You know, there's more to us than work—inspector verses entrepreneur. There has been from the very beginning, even though we couldn't acknowledge it."

"You mean you couldn't because you were there to spy."

"Right."

"Things haven't changed."

Cleo detached her hand from his. "They have, but I don't want to get into an argument about it," Taylor said.

Just then the credits for *The Josephine Baker Story* started and conversation stopped. Taylor recaptured her hand again and held it in his lap.

Cleo wakened to the sound of seagulls and the smell of coffee. After a shower, she dressed in jeans and an aqua top and went to join Taylor. His hair was ruffled and he was unshaven, he was the picture of a nineteenth-century sea captain.

"I picked up breakfast. There's a wonderful little restaurant down the pier. Thought you'd like to eat on board."

"I would, thanks." Cleo opened a styrofoam carton and peeked at pancakes and an omelet.

While she was distracted, Taylor took the opportunity to sneak a kiss.

"This isn't getting to know each other."

"Different techniques make life interesting. I've wanted to do that since yesterday."

"Well, if we're going to do this, we may as well do it right." Cleo put the food on the counter. She stood on tiptoe, linked her hands behind his head and claimed his lips. She heard a thump as he set the coffee down. Their tongues teased and toyed. What started out as light play quickly escalated. Before she knew it, she was plastered against the countertop, Taylor's long body pressing into her.

Cleo rubbed against him, liking the feel of his body after having longed for it for eternity. And the memories of that one night were never far away.

Taylor's response was to grip her behind in his hands, letting her feel the bulge in his pants.

"Umm. We can skip breakfast," he panted as his tongue swirled against her ear.

Cleo tried to pull back, but couldn't with the counter against her back. Instead she turned and handed his coffee to him. "Sip on this."

"I'd rather sip on you," he said taking playful sips from her neck.

"This is safer," Cleo said, holding the cup to his mouth, enjoying every bit of his touch, but not wanting to take on too much, too soon.

He didn't take the cup but merely sipped the drink as she held the cup, watching her as he sipped. His breathing was ragged. In a minute he relented and backed away.

With trembling hands and a thumping heart, Cleo eased past Taylor to set the table.

"Let's eat out on deck," he said as he leaned against the counter watching her. "You'll enjoy the view."

Cleo glanced at him. He was as calm as if nothing had occurred, while she was a mass of nerves and emotions. She nodded her head.

At noon, they left the boat and explored the island by foot. Their first stop was the marine museum, which they explored for two hours before they walked around more. The temperature was a little cooler than Saturday, but Cleo didn't mind.

When Taylor came out of his stateroom after his shower that night, he pulled up short. Looking sexy, Cleo was stretched out on the sofa reading a book.

If she thought that wearing a robe covering her from neck to feet would curtail the ardor in him, he could have told her differently. Smelling sweet after a shower, with her skin glowing, he couldn't resist bending over her head for one little taste of her.

She reached up to touch his cheek. That was all the incentive Taylor needed. He knew the delights to behold in her arms.

He reached for the opening of her robe and glided a hand inside, touching the warm skin waiting for him. The skin he'd dreamed of touching.

Her subtle fingers reached to caress his torso, their upside down position lending the perfect angle to touch and enjoy.

He leaned up to watch her slumberous eyes as they opened to gaze at him. Taylor leaned over further, kissing her collarbone, weaving a path to her breast. Pleasure shot through him to find her bare breasts. Then he realized he hadn't encountered a nightgown either. He bolted up, using both hands to pull the robe apart.

He basked in the sight of her and only her.

Taylor didn't need any other incentive. "Are you sure?" he whispered, hands trembling slightly.

She nodded.

He came around the sofa, hoping his moves were smooth. He was too filled with her to concentrate on practiced moves as he lifted her from the sofa. Any other man would find her frame to be heavy. At five-ten she was merely a nice armful for him.

Taylor headed for the stairs, squeezing past the narrow doorway, and realizing that both of them couldn't fit through together.

Regretfully, he lowered her to her feet.

Cleo laughed. "It doesn't make for stereotypical romance, does it?" she said backing into his stateroom, giving him inviting glimpses of her.

"Who'd have thought?" Advancing on her, Taylor realized the laughter gave him a moment to cool his ardor enough to pleasure her as she should be pleasured before the actual act.

When the back of her knees touched the bed, Cleo sat down. Taylor pushed her flat on the mattress.

"It feels like I've waited forever for this night," he said, gazing at her.

"Me, too." As he leaned toward her, her arms came up to encircle his neck.

Determined to take his time—to make it a memorable occasion for both of them, Taylor unwrapped her arms from behind his neck and slid down her body, kissing her along the way.

He stood ridding himself of his clothes, watching her naked, enticing form all the while.

Taylor bent and kissed her knee, flicking a tongue to the inside of her thigh.

Her soft moans drove him on. He brought a hand up her other leg.

As his tongue caressed her thigh, his fingers tangled in her intimate curls.

Her hips rose to meet his fingers as they stoked the heat in her. Her fingers tightened on his head.

Taylor kissed a path up her torso, giving attention to every sensitive point amid her moans and groans. He slid his body on hers finally kissing her sweet, hot mouth, relishing in the contrast of his hairy skin against her soft smoothness.

She pushed him on his back and kissed him, touching him until he was ready to explode.

Tumbling her on her back, he slipped on protection and glided himself into her, exhaling in ecstasy as her damp tightness wrapped around him.

He kissed her.

She stroked him.

They rocked to the beat of the tides until she tensed, singing the song he wanted to hear, and he had his own release.

The remainder of the weekend passed in a daze. Two carefree adults enjoying it to the fullest, knowing that the pleasure was temporary.

Cleo didn't sleep in the forward cabin again, even though she still used her own head and shower. The showers were too small for both of them to fit at once.

Even now, after showering that last night, Taylor leaned back on her bed, his hand behind his head following her every move.

"Ready to go?" she asked.

"No. I enjoy watching you dress."

"Last night when you did this, we didn't make it to dinner," she cautioned.

"Who cares about dinner?" Abruptly he sat up and pulled her against him. Kissed her.

"We do. I've got to reapply my makeup."

"Good, I like watching that, too." He kissed her neck. "I like your perfume."

The ride back to Washington was anticlimactic and quiet. Cleo sat at the helm with Taylor, he even taught her to steer. And she realized it wasn't as easy as it looked.

Through it all, he used every excuse to touch her.

Chapter 13

Rosebud limped through the door Wednesday morning.

"What happened to you?" Cleo asked putting down her package to rush over and assist the older woman.

"I can make it. I just went dancing last night. They had a swing dance contest."

Swing dancing was all the rage now.

"Looks like you outdid yourself," Cleo commiserated as she assisted the woman to a chair.

"But did I have fun!" Rosebud said as she gingerly slid in the chair.

Cleo laughed. "I bet you did."

"Don't get sassy, now, I can still outdo you with some swing, girlfriend."

"Well, you had best dream about that swing for a few days. Why didn't you stay home today? You worked the weekend for me." Cleo got the woman a cup of tea. "I wouldn't have minded. I expected you to after covering for me the last four days," Cleo admonished. "Sip your tea. I'm going to pour my cup."

Rosebud waved a hand. "It's better when I move around," but she stayed where she was.

"How did you get Albert away from his mother?" Cleo asked, curiosity eating her.

"I wondered about that. He says she's loosening up toward me."

"About time."

"I'm no threat. I won't be taking her baby from her. Enough about me. How was that boat trip, girl? Let me look at you. You're actually sparkling."

"Was it wonderful!" Cleo said dreamily. She described the yacht and trip in details. "I expected us to have to share the head and to sleep on a couch, but it has two nice size staterooms, one at each end." Cleo sipped her tea. "I couldn't live on one, but they're perfect for unwinding."

"Coming back spouting boat talk. You look rested. Better than I've seen you in months."

"By the time we reached Captain Bill's, I felt like a one-ton weight had lifted from my shoulders," Cleo sighed. "The air floating across me—not worrying about work. I need to do it more often," Cleo finished. "You were right."

"You're going to have to repeat that so I can tape it," Rosebud said. "Isn't that what I've been telling you? You need to take more time off. And although I haven't completely forgiven him yet, Taylor's just the one to get you away. He's scored a few brownie points with me."

"He's back in your good graces, then."

"If he can get you away from this store, there's got to be something good about him."

"He's okay," Cleo admitted, a warmth infusing her face with memories of their weekend.

"Um. And what about this weekend with Taylor?" Rosebud asked.

"He was okay. We got a chance to get to know each other." She looked away.

"Did you like what you discovered?"

"I did."

"So, what did you do?"

"We went to Solomons Island. Ate crabs for dinner. Toured the marine museum. Walked the city. Just tourist stuff."

"You deserved it."

"So have you. You get next weekend off, Rosebud."

"Now what am I going to do with a whole weekend off? Get real."

"Maybe swing dancing again?" Cleo asked.

"There is that," she sighed.

"Tell you what." Cleo went to a cabinet and pulled out a bottle of rosemary blend. "Take this and rub down in it."

"I already did. I'll put more on later." She limped to the cash register to open up.

"Have we received many new orders from the open house?" Cleo asked, all business now.

"They're stacked on your desk. They've been calling right and left."

"Good. I had moments when I wondered if anyone would show up. I think we'll do this every year."

"It was a good marketing tool. And you'll have something for Taylor to do while he snoops around here."

"Between the carpentry and his actual work, he's put in enormous hours the last few weeks. He needed to get away as much and I did."

"That will continue if you decide he's the one." Rosebud said eyebrows raised.

"We'll see." Cleo strolled to her office. The stack of orders was more than she'd expected. She plunked her tea on the desk and leafed through the orders, mentally calculating the extra employees she'd have to hire to get it all out before December.

She turned on the computer and pulled up the account for the first order and input items.

It didn't take long to fall into business as usual. Still, as she worked out her supply orders, she paused a few seconds a time or two to reflect on her weekend.

Sam smirked when he saw Taylor. "Good weekend?" he asked, bearing a cup of coffee.

"What happened in my absence?" Taylor said as he printed the data e-mailed to him about Cleo's case.

"Nothing from the mailboxes we're monitoring."

"We thought they were through with that one."

Sam lounged back in the comfortable chair the secretary had recently ordered for Taylor.

"You know, in that mailbox we found one or two names other than Cleo's. We can give Chicago a call and have them merge all their cancer cure data with similar traits like dollar amounts and see what pops out."

"We're limiting ourselves by focusing only on her," Sam agreed.

"Yeah. At the rate we're going, it'll be months before we get anything." Taylor wanted time to concentrate on Cleo and their relationship without the intrusion of the investigation. Cases such as this were a part of his daily routine, but he usually left his work at work, which was impossible with him dating Cleo.

"So, how are things between the two of you?" Sam broached the subject again.

Taylor wasn't about to divulge any personal information. "She's worried about the case and its effect on her business," he offered instead.

"You refuse to say anything about you and her."

"It's got nothing to do with this." Taylor wasn't going to be coerced into mixing business with pleasure. "Have you done the investigation on the accountant?"

"I sent it off on Friday. Should be getting something soon."

Cleo would pitch a fit if she knew they were investigating her friends, but they had to cover all the bases.

Taylor arrived at the store in the late afternoon. Cleo was closeted away faxing suppliers.

Rosebud and Tina were manning the store alone.

The phone rang and Rosebud answered. She buzzed Cleo in her office.

As always, the store was neat and colorful. Taylor gazed around the store as Tina assisted a customer. Her manner mimicked Cleo's. He'd been skeptical when she first mentioned the high-school mentoring program. Now, as he watched Tina's expert handling of the customer, he realized how important the program was for youth. By mentoring Tina, she'd taken Ashand and Bertrand under her wing.

It was more than simple goods that bought customers to this store. It was a gracious, attentive sales staff, the exquisite and colorful displays and arrangements, the promise of peace and serenity at night in a bath or at rest when enjoying the aroma of Cleopatra's Aromatherapy products. All these components bought customers through the door time and time again.

He sauntered into the office. Cleo had leaned her head on her hand. He stood by the door a moment just taking in the view of her. He could only see the blue blouse and wondered if she wore slacks or one of those short skirts. A royal-blue jacket rested neatly behind her chair.

Taylor approached her to massage her shoulders to loosen the kinks. She'd liked it when he did that on the boat. She'd probably been behind the desk most of the day.

When she heard him, she looked up. She opened her mouth to speak, then closed it tightly.

"You've been working too hard," Taylor said cautiously wondering if a rough day of work alone caused the strain on her face.

"It's more than that," she all but whispered.

"What is it?" he asked as he approached her.

"My main supplier is refusing to sell to me until this business clears up. I expected some fallout from this case, but not my supplier and not this soon." She got up to pace.

"Once this hit the news I hoped my name would be cleared and soon business would return to normal. But if I can't get supplies, I haven't got a business."

"How could they have learned that? My office is hush-hush about this case."

"I don't know, but I need supplies. A lot of them."

"The supplier isn't under investigation."

"But they don't want negative publicity reflecting on their business." She plunked into her seat.

"Try another supplier."

"I've got a huge order to get out. Their products are pure and the best. They can supply me with everything I need."

Taylor walked over to her and rubbed her shoulders. "There have to be more suppliers you can try."

"I could get the same response from them if they think I'm involved in fraud. A bad reputation can be the kiss of death. But I've got to try."

"That's the way."

"Until you find who's really responsible, I'm going to have all kinds of problems with my business."

She said it as though she trusted him to find these people. Taylor felt both strength and fear. Strength from her trust in him. Fear because he knew truth didn't always win.

"We'll find them, Cleo," *if it's the last thing I do,* he vowed to himself.

"It's a matter of getting everything I need in time."

She turned to her computer and opened a file. "I've got a list of suppliers in my directory. I may as well start calling." She scanned a file clicking on a name.

"Yeah, I'm leaving, but I'll see you at your house tonight."

Cleo nodded. Taylor wondered if she even heard him.

He hated feeling so helpless. They had to plod through one clue after another, never knowing when the right one would click in place. It had a time limit of its own. Simply because he wanted hasty answers, it didn't necessarily produce hasty results. The key was being methodical and thorough.

He went back to the office to shuffle through the case files.

As Cleo hung up the phone on another supplier who couldn't ship her enough supplies to fill her order, Rosebud floated into her office. She wasn't limping as she was earlier that morning. Moving about all day must have loosened her muscles.

"Things are slowing down, so I'm going home." She looked closely at Cleo. "What's wrong?"

"I've lost my supplier because of this business."

"Oh no."

"The problem is finding a good one and one who can supply us with all that we need in time to get these orders out."

"Cleo, this doesn't make sense," she said as she sat in the chair across from Cleo.

"I know it doesn't, but I don't have time to think through it right now. I've got to get my supply list out this week to get my products on time."

"Even if you were involved in fraud, it wouldn't reflect on them."

"It would if it involved their products."

"You don't sell vitamins or medicines."

"But it can tarnish their name, just as it can tarnish my business if my customers thought I was involved in fraud." Cleo rubbed a hand across her face.

"Who would do this to you?"

"The only connection is Mrs. Gross who owned the health-food store I worked at in college."

"But I can't see her coming back here where she could get arrested."

"She doesn't have to be here. That's the beauty of mail order and the reason the postal inspectors have such a hard time catching these people. She could be absolutely anywhere."

Cleo stood and paced the office. "When will it ever end, Rosebud? Why is it happening to me? And why now?" She blasted out in frustration.

"We'll get through this, Cleo." She got up and went over to Cleo to hug her.

Cleo held on to her as if she were a lifeline, needing that contact and knowing she couldn't afford to wallow in it for too long.

"Don't you worry." Rosebud leaned back and reached up to brush the front of her hair in a motherly manner. "What can I do to help?"

"Go home. Come in nice and fresh in the morning and enjoy your date with Albert tonight." She turned and walked back to her desk dropping down into the chair.

Rosebud waved. "That can wait."

"There's nothing you can do tonight. It's too late. I'll get on the phone first thing in the morning."

"You want me to stay with you tonight?"

"No. I'm going to find another supplier. It's just going to take some time. That's all."

"If you're sure."

Cleo grabbed Rosebud's purse, hugged her, and steered her to the door. " 'Bye."

Rosebud hugged her back. "Right is on our side, child," she patted Cleo's hand.

"Yes." But right didn't always win out, Cleo knew.

Taylor's car was parked in her driveway when she arrived home. Dressed in jeans, T-shirt, and an open windbreaker, he leaned against the car. At any other time, she'd reflect on how good he looked and plan how they'd spend their evening together. Now, she wasn't in the frame of mind to think of romantic evenings.

Cleo used the remote control to open the garage and drove in. Once there, she opened her door, squeezing around in the tight space. She grabbed her briefcase off the floor behind the front seat as he walked up to her in the garage, carrying a paper bag, the scent of Chinese food emitting from it.

As soon as she straightened, his lips met hers, backing her against the car.

Cleo dropped the briefcase on the floor and linked her arms around his neck, needing that kiss and physical contact more than she ever imagined.

He tasted like ambrosia after the overlong day.

Slowly, he swirled his tongue around her mouth, tasting every corner.

Cleo moved her hands to feel him. She wanted to experience the feel of him all over again. She felt his hips undulating against hers and his manhood growing against her.

Cleo moved her own hips wanting to feel more of him.

They stood there enjoying each other for a few moments before he pulled back, breathing hard, just gazing at her. "Hi," he finally said.

"Hi, yourself." Cleo panted, knowing her knees would give out any minute, they were so weak. She locked them to keep them in place. If her life depended on it, she wouldn't have been able to move. So, together they just stood, breathing hard. "Been waiting long?" she finally asked him.

"Just a few minutes. Any luck on finding a supplier?" he asked.

She shook her head. "Not any who can supply me with everything. I may have to use two or three." She pushed the remote control to close the garage and they entered the house together through the kitchen door.

"At least you'll get your order out. I bought Chinese to spare you a night of cooking."

"Thanks. Let me get rid of this stuff and I'll set the table."

He turned her toward the hallway. "I'll set the table while you pull yourself together."

Cleo pulled her suit off and hung it up on the door to air out, donned a robe, and went into the bathroom down the hall to splash water on her face and brush her teeth. She thought of how convenient it would be once Taylor completed her bathroom. She opened the door thinking of the colorful tile she'd picked out. Taylor stood there, his hand in the position to knock.

"I . . . I . . ."

Then she realized she hadn't closed the robe she wore. He clasped her around the waist, hauled her up against him and kissed her.

Cleo kissed him back, wanting him every bit as much.

"It was hard enough to let you go in the garage when I wanted to take you right there. Now . . ." he kissed her neck, backing her up against the doorjamb and rubbing against her.

Cleo relished the feel of him.

His hands stroked up her front, peeling the robe off her shoulders to let it drop soundlessly on the floor. Suddenly he lifted her and marched down the hall. This time they had no trouble getting through the door.

The cuddly, petite feeling Cleo experienced in his arms added to the sensual wave enveloping them. Settling her on her bed, he followed her down.

"My day just got better," Cleo smiled up at him, linking her fingers with his.

"You ain't seen nothing yet," Taylor said, nuzzling her ear, sending pinpoints of pleasure soaring through her.

She scored her nails down his back and whispered in a sultry voice. "All right, big boy, show me your stuff."

"Show you my stuff, hum?" he said, more than ready for the challenge. "I'll show you my stuff all right." His hands splayed on her hips, his fingers moving around in concentric circles until his thumb touched her most sensitive spot, flashing across and pressing, all the time moving. Her hips moved, seeking more, and she moaned, pressing closer to the delight.

Her senses spiraled, her hips undulating. His mouth closed on a nipple, laving it, nipping it in conjunction with his fingers pleasuring her. Her senses skyrocketed until she reached her peak, singing out her release.

She lay still, exhausted and drained, knowing the life had been sucked out of her until he moved up her languid body, kissing her breasts, stroking her thigh, slowly waking her sensitive nerve endings to more pleasures.

She pressed him to the side.

"My turn," she whispered.

He sprawled on his back giving her the opportunity to have her way with him. "Mr. Postman what do you want?" Her breath whispered over his skin. "Air Express, or Priority?"

He bucked beneath her touch.

"Priority, baby. I'm wanting it to last."

She kissed and touched, and nipped his body, inch by magnificent inch of sleek maleness.

She reveled in his long, fluid body, letting him know by touch how special he was to her, until he groaned, grasping for her.

She reached in the drawer, pulling out protection, sluggishly gliding it on as she stroked the magnificent length of him.

He tensed under her exploring fingers.

"I can't hang on much longer, baby," he moaned, his deepened voice strained.

"Just a little while longer," she teased.

"You like playing with fire don't you?" His fingers clamped on her thighs.

Finished with the teasing, she straddled his hips and slowly slid on him in teasing playfulness. His hips moved up to meet her sleek tightness, one hand gripping her hips, rolling them to please him and her, his other hand tugging her nipple.

Suddenly wanting all of him, she sank on him, loving the total length of him touching her deeply.

Her high-pitched moan matched his deeper groan. They moved in a cadence as old as mankind.

Their climax was explosive, leaving them exhausted and breathless.

Afterward, damp from the exertion, Cleo sprawled on top of Taylor, her breath catching.

An hour later, after a restoring shower, they wandered into the dining room. The only light visible was the warm glow from the rapidly melting candles.

"You've been busy," she said.

He merely smiled. "I'm going to work on your bathroom for a couple of hours tonight."

"Do you have the energy?" She took the food to the kitchen to reheat while he threw logs on the fire.

"You just supplied me with enough energy to last the night," he teased.

"Taylor, you don't have to do that," she said. It was too much to expect him to work all day and later work on her bathroom. Even after the shower, she was too languid to even consider work.

"I always finish what I start. I've got plenty of energy now." Moving around the table, Taylor held the chair for her and Cleo slid into it before he strolled around the table to take his own seat.

She caught a double meaning in that statement and wondered where their relationship would progress. But now, he was here, sitting at her table.

Cleo realized she wanted him close enough to touch,

not down at the other end of the table. But watching him from a distance had its own merits.

She just enjoyed the view as they ate their dinner by candlelight.

Chapter 14

"Cleo, good news!" Rosebud huffed into the office as Cleo started to make a phone call.

"What is it?" Cleo glanced up quickly placing the receiver on the hook.

"I had a date with Albert last night," she said catching her breath.

"You mentioned it." Knowing Rosebud's feelings about Albert, Cleo wondered at the excitement. The older woman dropped to the edge of a chair, her hands clutching her huge rainbow-hued tote bag. Her eyes sparkled and Cleo wondered if perhaps she'd finally fallen for Albert after all.

"Well, Albert's college friend works for a large aroma-therapy product supplier. He said he'll talk to him and he's sure he can help you out."

"What's his company's name?" Cautiously, a modicum of hope blossomed in Cleo's chest.

"A-First Distributors, he said. It guarantees pure products."

"I've heard it carries supplies from good suppliers, but I've never tried its products." She pursed her lips thoughtfully, trying to remember what else she'd heard about the place. She recalled that she'd thought of trying them once or twice but never got around to it.

"I can't think of a better time," Rosebud said standing to approach the closet to hang her coat. She moved much more freely today than yesterday.

"This could be just the break we needed." Deep in thought, Cleo inhaled deeply and blew the air out between her fingers. Hope made her light-headed.

"I gave Albert your number," Rosebud said as she approached the chair again. "He said he'll have his friend contact you today."

"As soon as I hear from him, I can work on scheduling packers. This friend is turning out to be quite useful, Rosebud."

"Now that we aren't romantically involved, he's okay to be with."

But he'd never replace Ronald. "Are you still getting letters from Ronald?"

"He calls at least once a week. His letters are sparse though. Usually a card signed 'Love Ronald.' I know I'm losing my mind, but I'm going to marry that man. He hates to write, but he's doing it to please me. That should count for something, shouldn't it?"

"Sure it does. Lets you know he cares."

Rosebud stood. "Well, if you need anything, I'll be in the shop.

Cleo started the computer and clicked on her order file. Even though she got good discount prices by using one supplier, she realized it wasn't safe going that route anymore. She needed to keep at least two in her repertoir, just in case.

* * *

Taylor entered her shop at ten, looking gorgeous as ever. Her heart always skipped a beat when he was near. She wondered how long this newness would last.

Cleo approached him and hugged him, her mind still reeling from the pleasure of last night and needing to share with him her morning's success.

"Okay what brought this on," he asked nuzzling her neck and nipping her ear. "Not that I'm not pleased with this response. I could get used to this, you know." His low whispery voice sent another thrill though her.

Cleo told him about the new supplier. "And I've given them my order. They can supply me with everything I need." Arm in arm, they walked to Cleo's office and closed the door.

Cleo avoided the chair behind the desk, electing to sit beside him in one the chairs facing her desk. "I've got some news, too."

"Yeah, what?"

"We've discovered that eighty percent of the people were on some kind of medication, whether it was drugs for hypertension or cancer medication. And they covered twenty states," Taylor told her.

"So, there must be some pharmacy connection."

"Or insurance."

"That's weird," Cleo shivered. "I know I hear about some kind of fraud or another on the news regularly. But I still don't see how people can sleep at night when they hurt others." She shook her head.

His hand caressed her cheek, his voice low. "Not everyone has a heart like you, Cleo."

"They don't have to be like me, just have a heart in

there somewhere." She said, pointing to her own heart. "Just care a little about other people."

Taylor touched her face again. "This world is too rough for you."

"There are more people like me than you realize. In your line of work, you just don't see enough of them, is all." She liked his casual touch. Not sexual, but warm and comforting and loving.

"Just keep reminding me of that, will you?" he whispered, leaning over for a kiss.

Cleo nodded and cleared her throat. "Take your heart for example. You must be exhausted from pulling double duty."

"I'm used to working long hours because of the moonlighting I did for years. Besides, normally we don't have to put in this much time."

Cleo knew he made light of his work, but she appreciated how hard he worked both day and night. Still, the atmosphere was too intimate for an argument. "So what's your next step?"

"We're checking pharmacies and insurance companies. Both of which span several states, so the research can take time. More time than we have."

"No reputable pharmacy or insurance company would involve themselves in petty crime after spending millions on research." Her hand absently caressed his arm.

"No, but that doesn't mean a greedy employee hasn't figured out a quick way to make a fast buck. Rarely can a company vouch for every employee regardless of the background checks."

"How can you stand doing this every day? It's wearing

on me, and I don't have to confront it regularly." When her hand neared his, they linked fingers.

"It's worse to stand by helpless, unable to do anything to help. This one is worse for me because it's personal. None of the other cases were personal. I did my job but, I wasn't dating the victim."

"Couldn't you get reprimanded for fraternizing with the suspect?"

He kissed her fingers. "You aren't a suspect any longer. Besides," he said as he lifted her on his lap. "How better to keep an eye on you?" he asked as his lips met hers.

His kiss was slow and leisurely, taking his time to taste every recess of her mouth. Cleo captured his face in her hands, loving the feel of him as his hands leisurely stroked her body, and they deepened the kiss.

"Is the door locked?" he asked.

"What?" It took a moment for his words to register in her fuzzy brain.

"The door . . ."

The ringing phone had them pulling apart abruptly. Cleo cleared her throat and leaned over the desk to answer it. It was Sam calling for Taylor.

"Yes?" Taylor asked, his voice low and thick.

"Watching the mailbox finally panned out. They caught a teenager getting mail from there this morning."

Taylor looked over the stubborn teenager who stood by the door. Tray was his name. He wore the usual teenager's clothing with the shirt twice his size and pants sliding so far off his hips that they looked in danger of losing the battle of staying up.

With the shoestrings undone, the tongue of his running shoes leaned back toward the toes and flopped with each step. A gold earring dangled from his left ear.

Taylor tried to imagine having a child of his walking in the house looking like that and couldn't picture it. Maybe it was a good thing he was single and childless. Though when he thought of Cleo, he wanted exactly what he feared.

Marriage and children. Maybe things would be better when his child grew up.

He didn't believe that for a moment. You could only raise a child to the best of your ability, love them, and pray for the best.

"Have a seat," he told Tray.

The teenager sauntered over to the chair and slumped into it.

Immediately, Taylor made comparisons between Ashand, Bertrand, and Tray. Ashand and Bertrand had goals and they worked hard toward achieving those goals. Taylor had grown to respect and appreciate those teenagers, and even though he'd made an error in judgment with Cleo, Taylor realized it was part of the package he signed on to when he became a postal inspector. She influenced these teenagers in positive ways.

A teenager like Ashand gave him the idea that there was hope for the future and children after all. Then too, he knew the media reveled in the disreputable ones. Too bad more focus wasn't placed on the good ones like Ashand, Tina, and Bertrand. He wondered at the difference it would make.

"I already talked to the other guy." Tired of waiting,

Tray finally broke the silence. He never took his eyes from his hands.

"I wanted to talk to you, too," Taylor said. "Do you have a problem with that?"

"I got nothing to hide." He dug his hands in his pockets and rocked on the back legs of the chair.

"Good. This shouldn't take long." Taylor leaned forward in his seat. "Exactly how did you get this job?"

Tray shrugged his shoulders. "Answered an ad in the local paper."

"What paper?" Taylor asked.

He held his hands up. "Man, I don't remember. I answered so many."

"Who interviewed you?"

"They called me. Sent me an application."

"And?" Taylor prodded.

"They called me back and said I had the job."

"You didn't think that was a little strange?" Taylor wanted to know.

"They paid good. I wasn't doing anything illegal. Just picking up mail for four weeks and mailing it on until they returned."

"And that didn't seem odd to you?"

"I pick up my neighbor's mail for free when they go on vacation. What's the difference. I'm getting paid now."

"How do you get paid?"

"I already told the other guy. I get checks in the mail," he said impatiently.

"What would you do if they missed a check?" Taylor asked. "You've got no way of contacting those people."

"I'd stop working for them."

"What do your parents say about this."

"My mom's glad I'm not on the street selling dope and stuff. I wouldn't get mixed up with nothing like that."

"How do they know you've mailed everything off? Do you call them?"

"No. I stash the letters in those two-day envelopes and mail them off. I'm honest."

And Taylor believed him. Wearing baggy jeans and scruffed-up sneakers didn't necessary indicate criminal behavior. Taylor knew how unfair stereotypes could be.

He got back to business. "They have no idea when your envelopes will arrive."

"My orders are to go to the box twice a week and mail the stuff off. They know when they're supposed to get it." He looked down at his hands again.

He was holding something back, Taylor thought. He let the silence swell in the room.

"Again. You don't call them to let them know the mail is coming," Taylor repeated.

"No."

Taylor turned the sentence around. "You don't write them to let them know the mail is coming."

Tray shifted in his seat.

"What was that?" Taylor asked.

"What're you on my back for? I'm not doing anything illegal. I've got an honest job, just mailing envelopes off to Minnesota. I told you, I'm not involved in drugs or nothing."

"I didn't say you were," Taylor said.

"Do you write them to let them know the mail is coming?" Taylor repeated.

He was met with silence.

"We need your help. Maybe you didn't know what

was going on, but you know something—unusual—is involved in what you're doing now. If not, you'd have a way to contact these people. They wouldn't have to go underground to get their money. You know this."

He swiped a hand across his face. "Man, I don't know what those letters are for. All I do is pick them up and mail them off. Nothing else." He looked around the room, his expression tense.

"Let me tell you about those letters. They contain five-, ten- and twenty-thousand dollar checks. These people advertise miracle drugs for terminal illnesses to people desperately seeking cures."

Tray's eyes widened.

"You're part of a criminal conspiracy and you're the only one we've caught, so far."

"I didn't know what was in those letters. I never opened any of them."

"Think about your grandmother. Think she can afford to lose thousands? What would happen to her if she spent her last dime desperately trying to hold on to life or a relative's life. That is what's happening to senior citizens all over the country."

"You can't blame me for that."

"Give me the address you mail a letter to." Taylor was getting nowhere.

Tray reached into his pocket and brought out a wrinkled slip of paper. It was another post office box.

Taylor looked up from the ragged paper. "How does this work?"

"I send an express mail letter to this address, letting them know a package is on the way."

"Thank you. That's it."

Relieved, the teenager left.

Taylor sensed Tray knew nothing of the fraud.

In less than a minute, Sam entered the room. "How did you know?"

"Just a guess. He had to have some other way of contacting these people."

"I'm putting someone on that new box."

Chapter 15

"Cleo, would you mind if we spend Sunday together on the *Serenity*?"

She paused, glancing at Taylor as she leaned to pick up their plates and glasses off the coffee table.

"I'll work on your bathroom Saturday and that night we can spend aboard. It's a little cold to cast off, but . . ." he left the thought unsaid.

She put her finger against his lips. "I'd love to spend Saturday night and Sunday on your yacht. Take Saturday off. You need the rest." Dark circles from too little sleep were underneath his eyes.

"I can't spend the day in bed."

"It's allowed on occasion," she teased.

"Tell you what, I'll rest with you Saturday night." A wicked grin followed.

And Cleo knew that grin held lots of possibilities that didn't include sleep. In fact, they'd get very little that night. But perhaps Sunday afternoon he could catch up on his rest. She'd see to it.

Cleo carried the dishes to the kitchen, packed them in the dishwasher, and joined Taylor.

They had fallen into the regular routine of spending evenings at her house. Taylor worked on the bath while she prepared supper.

Now, they sat on the floor, their cups of tea on the coffee table in front of the fire. Taylor seemed to enjoy the warmth on cold evenings. Cleo enjoyed snuggling up next to him on the sofa.

Still, he never left a change of clothing at her house. He spent the nights on his boat, even when he left late into the evening.

He pushed his coffee cup aside and leaned against the couch, stretching his legs out in front of him.

"Come here, please, I just want to hold you for a moment, all right?"

"Sure." Cleo slid next to him, and touched his face. "Is anything wrong, Taylor?"

"Nope." He turned just enough to nip her fingertips. "I just want to cuddle up with you. Nothing more." He tucked her head beneath his chin. "Is that okay with you?" he asked, his voice heating her as much as the fire.

"I love cuddling up." Cleo settled comfortably with him, running her fingers up his arm.

Their legs were entwined, and the room was lit by candlelight and the fire, Cleo nestled in his arm, lulled by the steady thump of his heart.

She could get too used to this, she thought.

Several quiet moments passed, each content with letting the effects of the day wash away as they gazed into the licking flames. "Tell me. How can you afford an expensive boat like *Serenity*?"

"You've waited a long time to ask me."

"I know."

"Carpentry work. I was perfect for this case because of it. I worked six years, investing every penny in stocks to save enough money for *Serenity*. And you know how the stock market has escalated in the last few years. My shares of Coca Cola and IBM soared. I got out of Netscape at its high."

"Where did you live before you moved on the boat?" She turned in his arms and her fingers busily stroked his chest, loving the textures of crisp hair against sinew skin and the steady thump of his heart.

"I have a town house in Springfield. When I moved onboard, I rented it out to a Navy couple stationed here for two years." His hand stroked her arm. "Everything that didn't fit on the boat went into storage."

"Why did you buy a town house and not the boat? You could have moved in it sooner."

"Because when I marry, I didn't want the money from my day job used for what could be perceived as a frivolous item. Who would want to marry a man with a boat and nothing more?"

Cleo declined to say that she would marry a man like him. She also realized the decisions he made were a part of his character she liked.

"So I didn't use any money from the postal inspector position for it. If I marry, I can sell the town house for a single-family house."

"You're an amazing man. Do you know that?" Comfortable in his embrace, she tilted her head and kissed his chin where stubble had started to grow.

He looked down at her and captured her lips. "You're an amazing woman."

*   *   *

The biting cold wind nipped and clung to Cleo as she and Taylor negotiated the finger pier Sunday morning. Her legs and feet were numb in her three-inch heels she had paired with a silk dress and black leather coat. They'd attended the eight o'clock church service.

"Let's change and walk to The Wharf for seafood," Taylor suggested as they stepped onto the *Serenity*'s deck. Though it was still cold, the covering protecting them from the elements made a tremendous difference in the temperature.

Still shivering from the cold wind, Cleo said, "Are you sure you want to walk?"

"Sure. It's only a couple of blocks. We'll dress in sweats. It'll get the blood pumping." He opened the door and they entered, the blessed heat inside the cabin immediately wrapping around Cleo. Grateful he hadn't lowered the heat before they left, Cleo quickly shucked her coat.

"I've got a taste for fresh tuna," Taylor continued. "It's nothing like the canned tuna."

"I've never had fresh tuna."

"You're in for a treat then."

They changed into sweats and down parkas to negotiate the cold again.

Cleo was surprised anyone was crazy enough to brave the weather for seafood, but brave souls marched back and forth, parking as close as possible to the stalls. No one lingered over selections.

"I can't believe I let you talk me into this."

"Invigorating." Taylor took her gloved hand in his

after he paid for the tuna and they strolled back to the boat.

"Have you had any results on the pharmacies and insurance companies yet?"

"No. Their security is working with us."

"If I wasn't swamped with work, I'd be biting my fingernails with worry."

"Trust me, Cleo. We're doing everything we can to get this solved."

She glanced up at him. "I know you are. I'm just so impatient." She watched the vapor produced from their warmed breaths hitting the frigid air.

"You're allowed but it takes time."

"I don't have much."

"An entrepreneur like you knows the value of timing." He squeezed her hand as they went through the security gates to the pier. Only half the residents lived on their boats year-round. Few ventured out today.

"In business I do, and I know what can happen if this lingers too much longer."

"This is my business. Trust me, Cleo." He put an arm around her.

Cleo nodded. She did trust him.

They put the fish in the fridge and Cleo convinced him to take a nap with her.

They'd slept two hours when the phone rang. It was Rosebud.

"Guess who's here?" she said to Cleo.

"Who?" Cleo rubbed her eyes.

"Your mother's here, kiddo."

"Let me speak to her."

"She's in the shower now. I'll have her call when she gets out."

Cleo got up. "I'll pick her up at your place."

"What is it?" Taylor asked.

Cleo covered the mouthpiece. "My mom's here," she told him.

"Have Rosebud bring her here. They can have dinner with us."

"You're certain?"

"Sure I am."

"Rosebud, would you bring her here and the two of you can have dinner with Taylor and me."

"Okay. I'll give you a couple of hours to pull yourselves together."

"Wear comfortable, low-heeled shoes."

"Don't worry, we will," Rosebud said and disconnected.

"I can't believe she just popped in without calling me. I could have picked her up at the airport."

"I'm looking forward to meeting her." Taylor rose from the bed, sluggish from fresh awakening, went to the bath and turned on the water.

"I'm going back to The Wharf to get more tuna," he said.

"Want me to go with you?" Cleo really didn't want to go. Even now, she heard the tides rippling in cadence to vigorous bouts of wind.

"No. Decide what you want to cook with the tuna. We've got potatoes and pasta. Fresh string beans and broccoli are in the fridge. Or we could go out. We're surrounded by excellent restaurants."

"I think she'll like it better here. We can all visit and not worry about having to leave soon."

When Taylor left, Cleo straightened the bed and made sure everything was in its place on the boat, which only took moments. She decided on baked potatoes, broccoli with cheese, and dinner rolls. They had nothing for desert.

Taylor brought back a lemon pie from a bakery and ice cream.

Dinner was almost ready when they got the call indicating Cleo's mom and Rosebud had arrived. Taylor went to the security gate to get the women.

Cleo watched them from the galley's window as they approached the Serenity. Taylor held both women's arms as they maneuvered the finger pier. They clutched his arm as if they feared if he'd let them go, they'd expire in the water at any moment.

Hattie Sharp wore a smart-looking burgundy pantsuit. The flower child days were indelibly erased from her forever. She was five-four and Cleo bent to hug her.

"It's so good to see you, Mom."

"You knew I couldn't stay away too long. You haven't come to visit me, so I have little choice."

"I promise to get away this summer. How long can you stay?" Cleo asked.

"Only a day. I'm meeting your dad in San Francisco for a business meeting. We're taking a week's vacation after and drive up the coast, I think."

"How is Dad?"

"Busy as always. I just needed to get away for some girl talk," she said looking around the boat. She turned to Taylor. "Young man, I don't know how you stand living on the water. The wind almost whipped me away."

Taylor put the women's coats on the guest bed. "I find the water relaxing. You feel the sway a little more on the end of the pier and today we're having strong winds, but I like having the unobstructed view."

Cleo realized the boat was swaying more than she'd ever felt it before. What a time for her mother to visit.

"You have a beautiful yacht," her mom said, continuing to look around.

"Thank you. I'll take you on a tour."

Cleo tended to the food while the three of them walked through the boat, talking all the time.

The dining area offered a beautiful view of the Potomac and Hain's Point as they ate dinner.

"You know, I saw a woman at the airport who looked exactly like Judy Gross. Except her hair was brown instead of black."

"Hattie, at least twice a year you see someone who looks like Judy," Rosebud said. "Remember that time you went chasing after this grandma through the airport who was met by her eight grandchildren?"

"And we all know Judy can't stand children," Cleo added thoughtfully. "Still . . ."

"I didn't say I saw her, just someone who looks like her," Hattie defended. "This woman was the same height, same brown coloring, but looked a little older than Judy would be. Some good-looking muscled man picked her up at the airport." When Rosebud started again, she pointed her fork and said. "I know, I know. She'd be a fool to come back here."

Cleo glanced at Taylor. He had stopped eating. "Did you get a look at the car he drove?"

"No. I didn't pay attention," she lamented. "I promised myself I wouldn't go chasing after that woman anymore. What good would it do anyway?"

Cleo hadn't mentioned her troubles to her parents. And she believed it could very well have been Judy at the airport. Under an assumed name, of course.

* * *

The supplies had arrived. This time Cleo hired the ladies from church to help with the orders. It was the first week in November. Cleo had two weeks before the rush of the Christmas season set in. She'd be in competition with other employers then. So she worked night and day, working double shifts on the orders to get them all done in time.

Working sixteen-hour days left little time to dwell on her problems.

It also left less time with Taylor, but since he spent at least an hour at the shop every day, the situation was tolerable.

She was still getting short-term loans for payments so at least she knew that her credit line was still good. Whoever was trying to ruin her business hadn't dipped into that.

Taylor dropped by her house almost nightly to work on the bathroom. She had a key made for him. Some nights he'd take her to the movies or a play. He insisted she take one day off each week. It was usually Sundays, and they toured the museums, wandering through like carefree tourists.

He was always on her mind.

He never mentioned tomorrow—what would happen once the case was solved, or once he completed the bathroom.

Cleo only hoped he was growing to care for her as much as she cared for him. Never in a million years did she expect to find love with him.

Even now, while she worked on orders, he was working on her bathroom. She wondered again why he didn't spend the night with her more often.

Cleo compared herself with other women who usually contemplated dates at nine on Saturday nights. Cleo usually worked.

It had been two years since her last close relationship, and she couldn't remember feeling an attraction this strong at that time. When they'd walked away from each other, neither of them ever looked back.

It wouldn't be that easy with Taylor.

"Cleo?" Rosebud called out.

"Yes?"

"I'm going to Greece for two weeks at the end of January. That'll give us time to do the inventory and I'll be back before Valentine's Day when the rush starts up again." She put a bottle on the shelf. "That man called me last night," she said referring to Ronald. "About to worry me to death. I finally agreed."

"That's great, Rosebud. What are you going to do about Albert?"

"We aren't intimate."

"You don't have to justify your actions to me. I understand. I get lonely sometimes, too."

"At least one good thing has come out of this separation. Ronald wants to marry me when he returns at the end of next year."

"I think he realized how much he loves you."

"And, about time, too."

"Yes, it is." Cleo went over to hug her friend. "Congratulations."

"Well, we've got work to do. It's time for the first shift to arrive."

"No need to worry. They're in the next room busily packing."

"Good. Time to open the store," she said brusquely.

The shop was closed and Cleo and Rosebud sprawled out on the chairs in her office.

Two weeks of double shifts, and the orders were in the mail on time.

"Rosebud," Cleo said sleepily, "I hope we never have to work that hard again."

"Un-uh. You'll say that until you get your next big order." Rosebud shifted to another position on the chair. "You hold that open house in September next year so we'll have some extra time on our hands."

"Customers will still wait until the last minute to place orders. It's just the natural order of things."

Even the peppermint still simmering in the room couldn't pump any more energy into them. It had worked enough to get them through the project, though. And Cleo was grateful for that.

They heard a banging on the door.

"I can't move," Rosebud groaned.

Cleo slipped her feet back into her low-heeled shoes and went to investigate. Probably Taylor. He'd dropped her off this morning.

It was Henry and his wife. Cleo opened the door to let them in.

"Hi," she greeted them.

"Just came by to pick up the files," he said, as they walked to her office. "Remember, Katherine and I are going to visit her sister for two weeks. I just wanted to make sure all the paperwork is up to date before we leave."

"Help yourself." She went to get an extra chair so Henry could take hers.

Rosebud had fallen asleep while she was out. Cleo wouldn't wake her.

"Your cousin's keeping the store for you this time?" Cleo whispered.

"Yes," Katherine answered in a tone as not to disturb Rosebud. "Otherwise we wouldn't be able to take so much time away. You've really been working poor Rosebud."

"Big shipment."

Cleo realized she hadn't taken a long vacation since she opened her store. The thought hadn't entered her mind until Taylor. Now, the idea of getting away for two weeks with him was exciting.

She wondered if they'd still be together in the spring when they could take the boat out again.

"Remember to go through the canceled checks while I'm gone," Henry reminded Cleo while he waited for his accounts to print out.

"I will," Cleo responded. She usually took a look anyway after he reconciled them.

She noticed that Rosebud still hadn't awakened.

"When will you leave?" she asked when she walked the couple to the door.

"Tuesday."

Taylor was at the door, looking good and smelling fresh out the shower.

He spoke to the Clarks and bid them good night.

"Your Jacuzzi is installed, madam." He kissed Cleo. "And your bathrooms are completed."

"I'm dying to get in the Jacuzzi." Cleo said, elated it was all done yet disappointed that his visits to her house would lessen now that he'd completed his work.

"You can do that tonight." He backed her into the store. "I was hoping we could try it together." His whisper against her ear sent shivers through her and wakened her in a way the peppermint oil couldn't begin to.

"Umm. Sounds good to me. Hold that thought while I get Rosebud."

The older woman was still sleeping and on the edge of snoring when they entered the office.

"I hate to wake her. She's worked so hard." Cleo touched Rosebud lightly on the arm. "Rosebud?"

"Umm," she moaned, repositioning herself to a more comfortable spot.

"Rosebud . . ." Cleo tried again.

Her eyes opened and she looked around. "Lord, I'm going to ache in every muscle I have after sitting in this chair." She straightened and shrugged her shoulders.

"We're going to take you home." Cleo went to the closet for their coats.

"I don't think I can wake up enough to drive. I'm not going to need my car anyway," she said as she pushed her arm through the sleeve of the coat Taylor held for her. "I'm going to sleep through tomorrow."

"Just don't show up for work until Tuesday."

"You don't have to ask me twice."

Cleo took her arm and strolled with her out into the brisk, chilled night.

"Hump. I'll wake up in this cold."

"You'll get back to sleep," Cleo said looking at the night sky. On Taylor's boat she could see millions of stars flashing. Here, with the intrusion of artificial light, she only glimpsed a sprinkling few.

Taylor ushered Rosebud into the backseat.

As Cleo rode home, she waited for the fatigue to return. Is it love that made the tiredness go away, she wondered? *Get off it, Cleo. You can't love Taylor. You're just enjoying dating him.* Then it struck Cleo that, even with work, he took the time to squeeze in visits to her.

Cleo went to the bathroom as soon as they entered the house and Taylor disappeared into the family room to light a fire.

The room was exactly as she'd pictured it, with off-white tile so she could change the color scheme at will. The Jacuzzi occupied the corner under the window, the shower behind it. Two sinks separated by large counter-space were along another wall. Taylor had even put the chair at the dressing table. She opened the door where the commode and miniature sink were closeted in a separate room.

And it was sparkling. He'd scrubbed all the surfaces. It only awaited her decorating touch.

Cleo went into the closet and pulled out the towels to hang on the warming towel bars. She placed candles in their holders around the room and sprinkled lavender in the fan, its scent immediately filtering into the room.

Then she sprinkled bath salts into the tub and turned on the water, soon returning to the closet, gathering odds and ends she'd purchased for the room.

Cleo undressed and put on her robe. She lit the candles and stood in the doorway to examine the results when she heard Taylor's footsteps approaching.

She looked up at him. He'd shucked his jacket. He

wore an Orioles T-shirt underneath it. "I love it, Taylor."

"This suits you. You're a romantic at heart." He approached her and lifted a hand to rub her shoulders.

"Umm," Cleo responded, reveling in his touch. "Workaholic Cleopatra Sharp a romantic?" she asked saucily.

"Look at your choice of business, woman. Essential oils, lotions, creams, bath-oil beads." He slid the robe off her shoulders.

Cleo faced him and pulled the T-shirt over his head, feeling his chest as she tugged on the fabric.

With Cleo's help he quickly undressed. Turning on the jets, they sank into the heated water. Warm water and bubbles surrounded them as they leaned back at opposite ends.

His hairy legs entwined with her smooth ones and their heads rested on bath pillows.

"It doesn't get better than this," Cleo sighed.

"Umm," Taylor groaned.

For long moments the only noise came from the jets, with the couple too languid to move a muscle, but enjoying the sensation of water pounding against them. The glow of the candlelights enveloped the room in romantic splendor. Cleo sighed and let the work of the last two weeks rub off her.

"What's happening on my case?" Cleo finally stirred enough to ask. "We didn't talk yesterday."

Taylor reached out a hand to stroke her calf. "We haven't isolated one company that's supplying names of people to victimize, yet. Every day we're getting complaints from people."

"Is it at least the same drugstore chain?"

"Different chains and different insurance companies." He looked at her a moment.

"What is it?"

"Did you know that Henry was suspected of embezzlement in the Children's Advocacy Group a few years ago?"

"No, I didn't," Cleo said. "I always go over my own books and he's never erred."

"He was cleared of the charges but we're just looking into everything surrounding you."

"He also worked for the government."

"True, and his record is unblemished there."

"Rosebud and I talked about Judy Gross. Though she'd be a fool to return here, she's a more likely suspect. You know it could have been her at the airport."

"She doesn't have to be here. I don't think it's one person but a group of people working this."

"Why?"

"It spans twenty states, and our data on this case goes back for more than three years. My guess is that someone in either a drug company or drugstore is getting the names and addresses of these people to defraud them."

"How are you going to find out who's doing this when they're using different companies? Do they have a person in each company?"

"It's not that many companies. We're gathering information and inputting it into the computer database. Then we'll do a search on comparable data."

"I guess any number of items could pop out, the same brand medication would only be one of them," Cleo said, wishing the situation didn't feel like pulling teeth to progress from one step to the next.

"Right." Taylor lifted her foot and massaged it. "Let's

leave business at the office for one night. I want to enjoy you.''

His voice lowered as Cleo snaked a hand up his leg, delighting in the feel of suds against hair and skin. And as Taylor's thumbs worked wonders on the soles of her feet, she forgot to worry about what would happen tomorrow.

He loved Cleo. But Taylor knew that with her proud nature, she wouldn't marry him until the case was solved. Taylor walked on the deck with his coffee and looked out over the water. All was too quiet without Cleo.

Since that trip to St. Solomon's Island, his yacht hadn't brought the peace and serenity he craved.

His bed was empty without her. The galley was too large without her around to bump into. Sitting in the salon was lonely instead of peaceful as it once had been.

Chapter 16

In his office, Taylor received a call early the next morning. An employee of Time Honored Pharmaceutical Marketing Company had been caught pilfering lists of names and addresses.

"Sam and I will be there as soon as we can get a flight out," Taylor said, then disconnected.

He glanced at his watch. Cleo was still at home. He dialed her number.

"Hello?" her breath was quick, as if she'd rushed to the phone.

"Hi yourself," Taylor said. "I have to leave town and I don't know if I'll return tonight or tomorrow."

"I'll miss you," she said. "Where are you going?"

"Chicago."

"Cold. Wear thick clothing. Have a good trip."

"I will," he responded, enjoying her concern.

If the interrogation turned out as he'd hoped, he would.

"I'll be thinking of you," he promised and hung up.

The secretary made plane reservations and he and Sam hurried to the airport to catch their flight.

Leaving the airport in Chicago, the weather was cold and rainy, but Taylor didn't mind. His life was on hold until this case was solved. If he had to suffer the harsh weather to move this case along, then he would. The quicker this case was solved, the quicker he and Cleo could make real plans for the future without his job hovering over them.

They went directly to the police station where a man named Marcus Pollar, had been charged with stealing company information. Time Honored insisted that it was illegal to take confidential information from the office. The man countered that he had taken the files home to work on. That it was done frequently by many employees.

He was lying and Taylor knew it, but it would be months and several lawyers tying up leads before the U.S. Attorney's office could prove otherwise.

Redheaded with freckles, Marcus was around five-six and trim.

The coldness in the man's gaze was enough to convince Taylor they finally had apprehended one person involved in the scam. He wouldn't care who he hurt. They used the "good cop, bad cop" routine, questioning him relentlessly to no avail. Then he'd insisted on a lawyer before he'd answer any more questions. His lawyer had him plead the fifth on everything.

Taylor called his office to have a background search done on the man.

Sitting at her computer, Cleo thought of the night in the Jacuzzi with Taylor. They'd had to turn on the hot water three times to warm up during their two-hour frolic. Her mind kept wandering between the Jacuzzi and canceled checks.

She wondered if he'd make it back tonight. Knowing that her mind wasn't on the checks, Cleo put them down and went into the shop to join Rosebud.

"I haven't seen much of Taylor lately, Cleo," she said as a customer left.

"He called this morning. He had to fly into Chicago today." She walked the aisles straightening products.

"Something with your case?" She stopped in the process of spraying glass cleaner on the case that held the cash register.

"He didn't say." Cleo shrugged her shoulders.

"I'm sure it is. He should have told you."

"He can't tell me everything about his job, I'm sure."

"This is different."

They worked companionably for a while, then Rosebud asked, "Did you finish your checks?"

"No, I couldn't concentrate. I'll return to them soon and then make the deposit."

"Look at the way you're moping around. How long did you say he'll be away?"

"I'm not moping," Cleo responded.

"Sure you are," Rosebud chuckled.

"I am not."

"You didn't go and fall for that man, did you?"

"Rosebud, I was smitten with that man from the moment I set eyes on him."

"Well, now. Maybe we can just fix up a little something to help you along."

"Essential oils can't make someone desire you."

"He already likes you. This will just prod him along."

Cleo sighed. "Prod him along to what? A prolonged affair?"

"So it's marriage you want now."

"In good conscience, I couldn't marry him with this cloud over my business. If word gets out and I have to start over again, I'll work long hours re-establishing it." Cleo sighed. "Rosebud, I won't have the money for a move."

"Don't do this to yourself."

"I could lose my house. You'll lose your job."

"All that isn't going to happen. You'll just have to wait and see. Besides you'll probably end up on *60 Minutes* or *Nightline* and have more customers than ever. You wait and see."

Cleo straightened one more bottle, needing to keep her hands busy.

"You're driving me crazy straightening bottles that

are already straight. Go take care of your checks." She led Cleo out of the store and immediately put lavender in the diffuser. That should calm her.

Cleo returned, "Whatever happens, I'm going to keep my business, Rosebud, and you'll keep your job. Don't you worry.

"We shouldn't have a problem with our corporate clients. They understand how criminal activity can reach innocent businesses."

"True."

"Didn't I tell you, you'll be fine? Stop borrowing trouble." Rosebud shoved her out again and she returned to her checks with a lighter heart. She still had several special order mixes to blend this morning.

With Henry on vacation, Cleo sat at her computer recording checks. She opened the envelope and took out the huge check from Bay Resorts. The experience was bittersweet. Sweet because it was the largest order she'd ever received. *And delivered on time.* Bitter because she still couldn't use her usual supplier.

Cleo scanned through the canceled checks, marking them off one by one.

After ten minutes, she checked the time. Wanting to deposit the check before the bank closed, she decided she'd work another half hour. By then Tina would be around to assist Rosebud.

She perused the check she'd mailed to A-First Distributors and thanked her lucky stars it came to the rescue.

At the ringing phone, she dropped the check and answered it.

"Cleopatra's Aromatherapy, how may I help you?"

"Cleo?" a sultry woman's voice she recognized responded.

"I need a supply of the relaxing lavender massage blend."

Cleo opened the spa's file in her computer and noted the blend. "You want the lavender, rose, and mimosa blend?"

"Yes."

Cleo used sunflower oil as the carrier oil in this particular blend.

"How many bottles would you like?" Cleo recorded the numbers in the file.

"Can I get anything else for you?" Cleo asked.

"No, Cleo. Thank you."

"I'll mail this in two days."

They disconnected and Cleo printed out the order and put it in the proper basket.

She returned to the check she'd dropped and realized it was turned on the wrong side. The unique scrawl of a signature captured her attention. Slowly, she picked it up and studied it. It was—it couldn't be. Cleo gazed at it some more.

She only knew one person with that deliberate slant. Even after nine years it was etched in her mind. She leaned back in her chair in disbelief.

She held the check up again. There was no mistaking that handwriting. It was as unique and as ornamental as the woman herself. Judy Gross did everything in extremes. Her dress, her makeup, her walk, her men. Everything, including her signature.

It wasn't a neat little flourish or an unreadable scribble. It was wild and fluid.

The woman had gotten off scot-free nine years ago.

To think she'd been practicing this chicanery, probably since the time she went into hiding. Cleo knew she was framing her because Cleo had the audacity to turn her in for fraud.

Cleo thought of Mrs. Ryker and hundreds of people like her who were plunged straight into poverty at the hands of this odious woman. Cleo and several of her friends had gotten together to throw a fund-raising drive for Mrs. Ryker. The local bank and several businesses had contributed money for her. Others had not been as fortunate.

Cleo almost shook in anger. She got up to pace in order to still the trembling in her hands.

She inhaled sharply and realized Rosebud had lavender oil in the diffuser—to calm Cleo, she realized.

She marched to her phone, ticking off what she needed to do. First, she'd call Taylor. Her hand hovered over the phone while still in thought.

Taylor was in Chicago today.

She had to do something. If not, Judy would get away again, leaving Cleo to hold the bag this time.

She dialed Taylor's number and left a message on his answering machine.

In a case like this, she couldn't afford to wait until all the evidence was gone. Cleo jumped up and rushed into the shop. She noticed Tina had arrived.

"Rosebud!" Cleo called out softly.

"May I speak to you a moment, please?" She turned and reentered her office.

Rosebud ran in, lifting a brow at Cleo's agitated state. "Yeah . . . what's wrong?"

"This check." Cleo waved it under Rosebud's nose. "It's from Judy."

At Rosebud's blank stare she said, "Remember the woman I worked for in college? The one fleecing those people out of money?"

"Yeah?"

"This check is from her. The company Albert recommended," she explained.

"Did you call Taylor?"

"He's in Chicago, remember?"

While Rosebud looked at the check, Cleo ran to the closet to pull out their coats, handing Rosebud's to her. "We've got to talk to Albert." Cleo tried to ease Rosebud toward the door.

"Come on, let's go. Albert works the night shift. He'll be leaving in a few hours. He should be home sleeping right now."

Cleo followed close behind Rosebud.

When they ran through the store, Cleo saw that Ashand had arrived. "Can you help Tina out until we get back?" She asked him.

"Sure."

"Thanks Ashand."

"Yeah, okay." He smiled.

When they pulled onto Oxen Hill Road, car horns beeped incessantly.

Rosebud cursed the delay.

"He'll help us once we tell him about the scam," Rosebud said.

"Perhaps we shouldn't mention the scam. Taylor doesn't want us to talk about it."

"That's before we got a lead."

The traffic was blocked because of an accident.

Cleo's heart was pumping. She realized she should

wait for Taylor. She trusted him, but she knew if she waited around, Judy would skip again.

When he arrived, she'd have already interviewed Albert, saving Taylor valuable time.

"Well, we just have to so *something*."

Up ahead they could see the policeman directing traffic. Cleo glanced at the clock on the dash and sighed, impatient to get on.

"Let's not mention the scam," Cleo repeated. "Let's let Taylor handle that. We'll just get information about this company."

Men were territorial creatures.

"All right, if you insist. Don't see what harm it would do. Looks like we can finally get through."

Only one lane was open and Cleo drove ahead.

In another five minutes they reached the apartment building.

She reached for her purse and realized that in her eagerness to speak to Albert, she had forgotten it. They caught him in the lobby as he was about to leave.

"I'm so glad we caught you, Albert," Rosebud said. "Can you come up to my apartment a moment? We want to talk to you."

He glanced at his watch. "Sure I've got a few minutes to spare." He looked at Cleo.

"Oh, this is Cleopatra Sharp. She owns the aroma-therapy shop I work in."

Cleo extended a hand. "Hello, Albert." She found him friendly and handsome.

"Good to meet you," he said as they shook hands.

They took the elevator to Rosebud's sixth-floor apartment.

"We wanted to talk to you about A-First," Cleo started as soon as they were seated in the apartment.

"What about it?" He crossed his right ankle over his left knee.

"I'm looking for a permanent supplier. Someone who can supply me with everything I need."

"It's a distributor who purchases worldwide. And the products are authenticated." Albert responded.

"It was only a small amount, but seals were broken on two of the bottles. I had to throw them away," she informed him watching his reaction.

"We . . . they guarantee all of the products. Next time send it back and you'll get a refund." He uncrossed his ankle and leaned forward, his elbow on his legs.

"Have they been in business long?" Rosebud asked.

Now that Cleo was here, she didn't quite know what to ask him without giving too much away. She realized she should have just waited for Taylor, after all.

"Seven years."

"I only have a post office box for them. Do you have their actual address?" Cleo asked.

"I'm sorry, I don't."

He seemed to know a lot about the company. And that bothered her. Did he work with it? Was he responsible for her problems?

And she wondered about the other woman. But Rosebud said she was in her seventies. Judy should be around fifty. A clinger didn't fit the description of Judy at all.

She'd let Taylor handle it from here.

Cleo stood. "Thank you for speaking with us."

Albert stood, also. "It was a pleasure meeting you, Cleo. I'll see you later, Rosebud."

When the door closed behind him, Cleo said, "Now, I'm getting bad vibes."

"I wondered why you didn't ask him more questions."

"He didn't seem to know where it is. That's what we really need to know." Cleo headed to the door. "Come on. Let's go."

"All right."

"Rosebud, I got the feeling Albert was holding something back. That he was actually part of the company."

"Why? I don't know. He knows a lot about its policies. And . . ."

"You don't have to work for a company to know its policies. I know the policies of companies I order things from."

"I know. It's just . . ."

"Do you think his mother could be Judy Gross?"

Cleo shook her head. "No. Judy is flamboyant and outgoing, not clinging."

"Just tell Taylor your suspicions. He'll look into it."

When they returned to the shop, Taylor was there.

"Did you get my message?" she asked.

"No," he smiled gathering her close. "Did you miss me?" he kissed her neck.

"No, nothing like that." She gave him the canceled check.

"Most companies stamp checks on the back with 'For Deposit Only,' stamps. It's odd that she wrote out this one."

"We'll check this out." He picked up the phone to call Sam.

"We went over there earlier."

He put down the phone.

"You did what?"

"Albert didn't know much. He told me that he only went to college with the owner. He didn't know the address or anything. You've got to move fast before you lose them again!"

"Don't you ever do that again! How do you know Albert isn't involved and you've just tipped him off?"

"We didn't mention the scam. I just told him I was thinking of using them as my exclusive supplier. But Taylor, he said something strange. When I asked him about guarantees, he slipped and said 'we' then corrected himself and said 'they.' "

"That's why you should leave the interrogations to us. We know what we're doing."

"You weren't here."

"You could have waited. These aren't your everyday mail-order suppliers you're dealing with."

He picked up the phone again and spoke rapidly to Sam. He turned to her. "What's his address?"

Rosebud rattled it off.

"I'll meet you over there," he clipped to Sam after he repeated the location. He spun around, heading for the door.

"I'll talk to you later." he snapped. "And stay away from Albert."

"Well!" Rosebud said. "We really blew his fuse."

By now, his high-handed attitude had Cleo burning with anger.

Without Rosebud and her, he wouldn't have anything.

Taylor knocked on Albert's door and waited. His gut instinct told him he wouldn't get an answer. After a minute passed, he knocked again. He heard no stirring within or footsteps approaching.

"Why doesn't this surprise me?" he asked Sam, not expecting an answer.

"They're searching for the owner of that box," Sam said. "Maybe we'll get an address on it."

An older man approached and unlocked the door across from Albert's. Taylor realized that apartment with the keyhole would make a perfect stakeout on Albert's apartment.

"We'll put Rosebud with a sketch artist," Taylor said after the man closed the door. "I'll call it in to have this place watched."

Taylor left, thinking that if Cleo had waited instead of acting emotionally, they'd have Albert for questioning. By now the man could have taken the necessities and be long gone, never to be caught.

He called into the office for a background search on Albert.

Taylor marched through the door, his stride brisk. He plunged his hands into his pockets as he confronted Cleo.

She tilted her chin and faced him straight on. "What happened?"

"We don't have enough on Albert to get a subpoena. Tomorrow, we'll get the address of the owner of that post office box. And we'll go from there."

"But what if he shows up there?" Cleo asked, frightened that they were leaving room for escape.

"We've got people watching that building to see if he or the woman shows up." He swiped a hand across his face and dropped into the overstuffed sofa. It had been a heck of a long day.

"Why don't you trust me, Cleo?"

"I trust you," Cleo assured him.

"No you don't. If you trusted me, you would have waited until I arrived to make a move." Disappointment flashed across his face.

"If I didn't trust you, Taylor, I would have mentioned the scam." She tried to placate him.

"You know I asked you not to." Exasperation followed quickly.

"Which is why I didn't. Now stop trying to second guess me. Have you had supper?"

"You're evading the subject." His day had been darn frustrating and getting worse by the minute.

"I've been in this situation before."

"So you've probably warned them so they could get away again," he said, disgusted, and underneath it Cleo caught—could it possibly be hurt?

"I didn't think that Albert was involved, just his friend's company."

"And you don't think friends warn each other?"

"We could argue this all evening. I apologize, okay? But I didn't give anything away. He thought I was just asking about a prospective supplier."

"This situation warrants more than an apology, this involves trust. You don't trust me."

"Here we go again. I trust you. I don't necessarily trust the authorities," Cleo snapped.

"I'm one of the authorities, remember?"

"Look, my business is on the line here, my bread and butter, my life. I have to do what I believe I can to clear my name."

"Don't you think I'm doing that?"

"This is a job to you."

He leaned back as though she'd punched him. "Is that all this relationship is to you?"

"Of course not. But I know that once this is over I . . . I don't know what happens. We never discuss it."

"Wham, bam, thank you ma'am?"

Cleo dropped into the chair across from him. The chasm between them was growing wider and wider, and at the moment she wondered how it had turned so bad so soon.

"I thought you felt—something for me."

"I do. I wouldn't have taken the trip with you or . . ." she shrugged her shoulders. "You've got to understand. The last time, there wasn't anyone to help us. Being in an interrogation room, not knowing what the outcome would be, no one there to protect me, was a nightmare. I needed to do something—anything—I . . ."

"You aren't alone in this. I thought you knew after the trip how I felt about you."

"We never discussed our feelings. Once the bathroom was finished, I didn't know if you'd continue to come or how often you'd come. We don't talk about us."

"If you were afraid, you could have spoken to me about it. You really have a high opinion of me, don't you?"

"Look, Taylor. We haven't had dinner. Both of us are frustrated and we're taking it out on each other. Why don't you relax while I put dinner on the table?"

"Typical female response."

"Typical male reaction. Soon, we'll be calling each other dirty names."

He sent her a frustrated glare.

Cleo marched to the drawer and plucked out lavender oil and shook ten drops in the diffuser.

When Taylor smelled it, he said. "And that silly oil isn't going to calm me. I've got a right to be angry with you," he shouted.

"And I've got a right to protect myself." Cleo ignored the rest of his tirade and set the table.

Chapter 17

When Rosebud entered the shop early the next morning, she greeted Cleo with, "How did it go with Taylor last night? Was he angry?"

"Yes. And he's angry at us for going over there," she said telling Rosebud the details while Rosebud hung her coat in the closet.

"Oh, that's just male posturing. You've just got to pet him a little. The caveman instinct still runs strong." Rosebud's hand was wrapped around a cup of tea.

"It's more than that, Rosebud." Cleo needed a cup of chamomile to soothe her.

"Not really. Even though he didn't trust you, you were supposed to trust him at all costs."

"I do trust him. He just wasn't around and I just wanted to get some information before he arrived." It all sounded reasonable to her.

"Take it from me and take the blame to ease his ruffled feathers."

"He's a grown man, Rosebud. And I still don't know

how he feels about me. He got insulted when I asked him about it last night." Cleo's hand tightened around her purse string as she remembered the conversation.

"Love can make you stupid, child," Rosebud said, disgust clearly ringing from her. "Can't you tell that man is as in love with you as you are with him?"

"I never said . . ."

"Oh, hogwash. Don't pull that on me. I'd have to be blind not to see it."

"Rosebud . . ."

"Just put some lavender into a diffuser to calm him after he gets back. Light a few candles. Put on a sexy nightgown, but don't be obvious. Pet him up a little—a lot. Say "yes" to everything he says and the rest will take care of itself," Rosebud assured her.

"I tried the lavender. He knows what it does and told me it wouldn't work on him," she continued. "He did mellow a bit before he left," Cleo said heading to the kitchen.

She wasn't about to pet him up or any of the other things Rosebud mentioned. They'd discuss this like rational people.

Rosebud followed her while Cleo poured her own tea.

"Did he talk to Albert?" the older woman asked.

Cleo told her what had transpired.

"The post office box they located belonged to the woman who must be Albert's mom," Sam said standing in the doorway. "The address given was the apartment we visited last night. And these people didn't get social security numbers until seven years ago," he continued.

Taylor almost reached for the phone to call Cleo, but he didn't. He'd wait until after the search and talk to her.

Instead, he called the U.S. Attorney's office and donned his coat. On his way to pick up the subpoena, he thought he couldn't help but be proud of a woman with Cleo's tenacity.

He considered what he would have done under similar circumstances. He wouldn't have waited for someone else, especially if that someone was halfway across the country. He would have gone to gather information as Cleo had.

Cleo wasn't a woman to wait for another to do for her. She took the lead. And that was one of the many facets of her personality he liked.

Taylor and Sam drove through the midday traffic to Gill Thacher's office and picked up the subpoena and headed for Albert's apartment.

They knocked on the door. Taylor didn't expect a response this time either. He had a gut feeling they'd left town.

Sam got the apartment manager to open the door for them.

Once in, they noticed the apartment looked as if the occupants had only stepped out for a little while. No evidence of hasty packing was apparent. The furniture and curtains were expensive, with colors of bold mauves and purples. Taylor didn't think it would appeal to a woman in her seventies.

Pulling on his gloves, Taylor pointed to the left and said, "I'll take the bedroom on this end."

Sam went in the opposite direction.

The huge mirror above the bed was the focal point

of the room. The furniture wasn't nearly as expensive as that in the living room.

Covers were thrown back on the unmade bed. A beer can stood on the bedside table near the lamp. Small change lay scattered on the dresser along with nail clippers and the electric bill. A pair of jeans was thrown haphazardly across the arm of a chair. Weights lay on the floor by the window.

Taylor pulled open the closet door. Inside were several neatly hung suits. Several shirts, fresh from the cleaners covered the shelf. Slacks and casual sweaters draped hangers. And row upon row of shoe boxes littered the floor.

Taylor took the tops off the boxes to make sure only shoes were in them.

The dresser drawers held only more clothing. Taylor was inspecting the last drawer when Sam appeared.

"I think you'll want to see this, Taylor."

"What is it?"

"Looks like the woman who lived in the other bedroom had a dual personality."

Puzzled, Taylor entered the room. The bed was neatly made, the bedspread a mauve floral pattern. Perfumes and a hairbrush with brown hair in the bristles sat on a mirrored tray on the dresser. A walking cane was propped against it.

On a Styrofoam head lay a gray and white streaked wig fashioned in a bun, the kind an older woman would wear. Even an older woman would wear something with a little less gray, Taylor thought. And it didn't match the hair in the hairbrush.

Taylor knew immediately that the wig was of good quality.

"Looks like Mama left without her hair?" he said.

"It gets even more fascinating. Look in the closet." Sam opened the door open.

One end of the closet had granny dresses, shawls, an old coat, and orthopedic shoes. The other end held smart colorful suits and dresses, blouses, skirts, three-inch heels, and several leather and wool coats.

Taylor peered at the queen-size bed. "Cleo says only Albert's mom lived with him. Looks like she isn't his mom, after all."

"That's what I thought," Sam said.

"Taylor pushed the hangers toward one side to get a better view of the back of the closet. He spotted two large boxes stacked in the corner. He bent and pulled them out. They were taped up as if to be mailed to a relative.

"Let's see what we have here." Taylor gave the top box to Sam and he took the other and ripped off the tape.

A double row of sweaters lay neatly stacked. Taylor took them out one by one. Wrapped in the last sweater was a zippered portfolio. He opened it and dumped the contents on the bed.

"There's nothing but clothing in my box," Sam said.

"We've got more than clothes here."

He picked up one of two bundles wrapped with white paper and held together with a rubber band. Sliding off the rubber band, he pulled the paper aside.

A two-inch-thick bundle of hundred dollar bills lay inside.

"Looks like we keep something around to prepare for all occasions," Sam commented.

The other bundle held the same. There were also

some twenties and tens in the portfolio, along with bank accounts and what looked to be offshore account numbers.

"Pay dirt," Taylor said with a smile that quickly disappeared when he realized that these people may have skipped and may not return for the goods.

"We'll set up a watch."

It was after five when Taylor left his office that evening. He thought of how he'd love to sink into Cleo's Jacuzzi with her after work. Instead, he called her, offering to bring over dinner for her. He'd never returned the key he used while renovating her bath.

Taylor picked up Chinese on his way. He showered and started a fire in the fireplace and set the place settings on the cocktail table in front of her couch.

Around the time she was due home, he lit the candles in the room and turned out the lights. Two minutes later, he heard her garage door open.

"Taylor?" She called once she entered the kitchen.

"In the family room."

Quick footsteps followed his voice. She stopped when she reached him, looking around in surprise.

"Had I known this greeted me, I'd have come sooner," she said.

Taylor slid her coat off her shoulders, sneaking a familiar kiss in the process.

"Hi," she said.

"Hi yourself. I could get used to this."

"Good." She looked puzzled at his statement.

"Hungry?" he said.

"Famished."

They shared meat appetizers of dumplings and shrimp tempura. Their meal consisted of crispy chicken, and to satisfy Taylor's desire for something hot, kung pao shrimp.

"I'm so stuffed I can't move," Cleo said afterward.

"Then don't." Taylor kissed her forehead and rose, taking the dishes to the kitchen. He stacked them in the dishwasher and poured fresh cups of tea before joining her by the fire.

This time they laid on the couch spoon fashion and talked of inconsequential matters as they gazed into the fire, his arm tucked comfortably around her.

"We made some progress today." He finally broached their findings.

She stiffened. "What happened?"

"We believe the woman posing as Albert's mother is actually your Mrs. Gross."

Cleo sat up. "What!"

Taylor eased her back in his arms and explained the two styles of clothing, the getaway money, and bank accounts.

"No wonder she always complained when Rosebud arrived. She's Albert's woman, not his mother. That's really sick," she tensed. "What if Rosebud had fallen in love with him? This would have broken her heart."

"Well, she's not in love with him. That's what counts."

"She'll blame herself for my troubles."

"She shouldn't. It's not her fault. With or without her, the results would have been the same."

"That's true, but I only hope she believes that," Cleo agreed.

"Cleo, we never got an opportunity to talk about my trip."

"No we didn't."

"We got a call from one of the pharmaceutical marketing companies we're investigating. Their security caught an employee named Marcus Pollard pilfering files."

"That's how these people got those names?"

"That's what we believe, though he wouldn't admit to it," Taylor said.

"Of course he won't," Cleo said. "They'd lock the doors and throw away the key."

"It's up to us to prove it."

"And you will."

"Pharmacies send in names and addresses of people who take certain medications. The marketing company only uses it for advertising purposes, which is legal and okay, but we believe this guy Pollard is using the same information to commit fraud." Taylor shifted to a more comfortable position.

"My goodness, Taylor, do you realize the number of people he has access to?"

"Sure I do. They get enough names to keep them in business for years."

"Which is why they can afford to leave mail unopened."

"Yes," Taylor agreed. "They get a fresh supply every month."

"This is even bigger than I thought."

"And probably involves more people than we've thought about," he said.

She stroked his face. "When you finish this case, it will really look good on your record."

"If I can prove it."

She squeezed the hand around her waist. "You'll prove it. I have complete confidence in you."

He nuzzled her neck. "That means more than you can imagine."

"I've always trusted you. That shouldn't be a surprise."

He squeezed her in reply.

"Judy Gross really expanded her business from nine years ago, didn't she?"

"It certainly takes advertisement and expansion to a new level."

"Taylor?" Cleo shifted.

"Yes," he answered.

"We need to talk about our relationship," she began cautiously.

"I'm not going to walk away from what we have when this case is over, okay?"

"Sure." Cleo was disappointed that was all he offered but wasn't ready to leave the topic altogether.

"Have you thought about having children?" she asked.

He rubbed a hand along her abdomen. "Yes, I've thought of it."

"Well, do you want any?" Cleo waited with bated breath.

"One day. One or two."

"I love children and I don't want my child to be an only child. I always missed having a brother or sister, someone who will belong to you no matter what."

"I'll belong to you no matter what."

Cleo pondered that. How can he belong to her if he wasn't willing to make a lasting commitment?

* * *

When the phone rang at four that morning, Cleo and Taylor, still wearing their street clothing, were asleep on the sofa. The fire had burned to ashes and the candles were barely a flicker in their ceramic holders.

"I left the office your number," Taylor said. "Let me get that." Groggily he stood and trod to the phone.

He cleared his throat. "Taylor here," he answered and waited a few seconds."

"We just spotted a cleaning lady with a vacuum coming to clean the hallway. She just happened to have a key to the surveillance apartment."

"Is she alone?" he asked.

"Yes. We're going to let her get in the apartment before we apprehend her," Sam said. "Thought you'd want to know." He disconnected.

"I've got to go," Taylor said to Cleo, placing the phone on the hook. "Got an extra toothbrush?"

"Yes." Cleo went down the hall to the bath and quickly pulled out a washcloth and toothbrush.

She sat on the edge of the Jacuzzi watching Taylor as he freshened up.

"Someone showed up at the apartment?" Cleo yawned, covering her mouth with a hand.

"Yes, a supposed cleaning lady," he said as he put lotion on his face. "In the middle of the night. Gotta go."

Taylor raced to the closet to grab his jacket. "I'll talk to you later," he said thrusting his arm through the sleeve. "Go back to bed." He neared her and kissed her on the lips as if he couldn't help himself, then turned and rushed out into the cold morning.

The cold air rushing in had Cleo rubbing her arms. She locked the door. After closing the fireplace damper, she noticed all the candles had burned out.

She went to her bedroom, pulled off her clothes, and snuggled under the blankets.

Cleo jumped every time the phone rang the next day.

"You're making me jittery. Why don't you go home?" Rosebud said.

"I'll just pace and worry."

"Well, what do you think you're doing here?"

"Pacing and worrying." Cleo had already rearranged files, recorded checks, made the daily deposit, and now she was dusting shelves in the store.

"Pretty soon, you're going to clean what you've already cleaned," Rosebud said, shoving a cup of chamomile tea into Cleo's hand. "You're going to wear yourself out if you don't sit down."

"Thanks. But I think a call from Taylor is the only thing that will calm me right now." She took delicate sips of the tea anyway.

"I hope he gets those people. They deserve whatever befalls them for what they've put you through."

"I hope he gets them, too, Rosebud. Especially for using you."

"Sick, I tell you. They're just sick."

Rosebud had taken the news of Albert and his "mom" rather well. She'd been stirred more by anger than any other emotion.

Cleo tidied the storage room before Rosebud and Tina grabbed her coat from the office to push her out the door at four. The doorbell jingled and of all people, Ronald walked in.

"Ronald?" Cleo said, first disbelieving that Rosebud's friend, all of six feet and solidly built stood before her. His black hair was cut close. And he had the solid muscles of a man who often worked out. He wore a beige sweater over stonewashed jeans.

"It's me," he answered. He went to Rosebud with a silly grin on his face, caught her up in a big bear hug. "Hi Bud," he said as he set her back on her feet.

"Well, my stars." Flushed, Rosebud patted her hair and looked down at her dress. "This is a surprise."

Cleo knew the woman wished she'd worn something more flattering.

"Got a couple of days leave and decided to take a short trip. We only got two days together before I go back. Think you can get some time off?"

"Sure she can," Cleo responded, knowing it was the perfect opportunity for them to clear up some of their problems. She handed Rosebud her coat.

"That store out there looks good, Cleo. Pretty and plenty of space. Just what the women like."

"Thank you, I think."

"You glad to see me, Bud?"

"Yes, I am. You could have called though. I would have met you at the airport."

"I wanted to surprise you."

"Well, you certainly succeeded," was her gruff reply, softened with a smile.

"Call me if they make any arrests, Cleo. I want to know what's happening."

"Arrests?" Ronald asked. "What arrests?"

They told him the gist of what happened without mentioning that Rosebud dated Albert.

"Tell me about this Taylor," Ronald demanded, in an aggressive stance with hands on his hips.

Rosebud and Cleo rolled their eyes and thought, *men*. Always controlling, always suspicious.

"He's my friend. And he's investigating the case. Not to worry."

"Are you sure you can trust him?" He relaxed, his arm inching around Rosebud's shoulders as he looked down at Cleo.

"Yes, I'm sure," Cleo said. "You and Rosebud go home and enjoy your two days together."

"You're like Rosebud's little girl," he said. "That'll make you mine, too. I think I need to check this Taylor out."

"If you've noticed, I'm not little anymore, Ronald. Rest assured Rosebud has already checked him out. Thanks for your concern, though." She put her arms around both of them and walked them to the door. "Enjoy yourselves."

"Hold it." He threw up a hand. "As much as I want you to myself, Bud, I'm thinking maybe we need to have dinner with Cleo and this Taylor so I can check him out."

"I'd love to have you to dinner, but I'm sure you want to spend your time with Rosebud, not with Taylor and me."

"This couldn't have happened at a worse time, but family's family. I've got to do my duty. We'll get together for a little bit tomorrow night."

"Ronald . . ."

"Don't forget to call," Rosebud repeated on her way out the door.

"See you tomorrow." Ronald snuggled Rosebud under his arm as they left.

On her way home, Cleo stopped by the supermarket to get salmon. She usually liked to get it from the fish market on Maine Avenue, but in her state of mind she wasn't about to tackle the rush-hour traffic for fish.

She cleaned, made a fire in the fireplace, cooked, showered, and set the table in the dining room in hopes that Taylor would stop by.

Each time she heard a car near her house, she rushed to the window to see if it were him.

Finally he arrived at eight looking tired and worn out. She noticed that, at some point, he'd showered and changed clothes.

Taylor merely gazed at how enchanting Cleo appeared, with the warm glow of candles in back of her and the ever present lavender wafting from a diffuser.

"Let me take your jacket," she said.

Taylor had forgotten he had it on.

He peeled it off and handed it to her. She disappeared a moment to hang it in the hall closet. The atmosphere was so inviting. How he'd love to come home to this every night. If they married, he knew he wouldn't be greeted with nightly scenes like this. But occasional episodes would suffice.

"It's been a long day."

"Was the woman Judy Gross?" Cleo asked. In silent agreement they walked to the couch.

"Yes, it was. At first she wouldn't divulge any information, but faced with taking the rap for everything, she opened up." Taylor pulled off his shoes and stretched out his legs.

"No loyalty among thieves."

"Not this one, anyway."

"What happens now?" Cleo asked, facing him.

"We were fortunate that although she wasn't one of the top people, she's hoarded notebooks of information for years.

"She even had a lawyer already picked out, which is one of the reasons it took so long. She wouldn't talk unless he was present."

"She'd stolen enough money to pay for the best. I'm sure." Cleo declared.

"She was facing years in prison. Her lawyer worked out a deal with Gill Thacher to get leniency."

"I can't believe this. This woman steals millions and she can work out a deal?"

"That's the way it works. She still gets time, and the government gets bigger fish than her. In this case the fish are a lot bigger, so I guess it's worth it."

"It also diminishes what I've been put through, what Mrs. Ryker has suffered and thousands like her."

"I know it's not fair, Cleo. But she'll still serve time. Just a lesser sentence."

"So she can get out to do it again?"

"That's the way the system works," Taylor explained.

"Who is this big fish?"

"Remember Marcus Pollard I mentioned the other night?"

"Yes."

"Well, he's one of them. He actually planned the pharmaceutical scam. She had conclusive evidence."

"What else?" Cleo asked.

"Cleo, this woman has a safety deposit box with information on the people she's worked with for the last ten years. It'll take the team weeks to get through it all."

"I see you're pleased."

"Cleo . . ." he started.

She held up a hand. "I'm sorry if I'm not responding the way you want me to. But this lady touched me and people I care about. Not some unnamed person in a ledger."

He rubbed her shoulders.

"And I don't want her getting leniency. I may not be very sophisticated, but it's the way I feel about it. She's just as responsible as Marcus Pollard. It was Judy who used my company name. Marcus Pollard wouldn't have thought of it because he didn't know me."

"Cleo . . ."

"And in a few years, she'll be out to exact revenge from me again." Cleo got up to pace.

"She'll be watched."

"I'm not that stupid. She would have served her time. She'll be free to go where she wants to and do what she pleases. When this hits the news, I'll lose my customers. I don't have their marketing techniques."

"Cleo . . . I . . . I just don't know what to say to you."

"There's nothing you can say. You've done your part."

A strained silence filled the room.

"What about Albert?" she asked.

"Her boyfriend. You and Rosebud spooked him. She doesn't know where he is."

"I told Rosebud everything I knew last night. At least she's taking it well."

"I'm glad," Taylor said, walking toward her.

"Ronald is here from Greece."

"That could be interesting. I take it he doesn't know about Albert."

"No, he doesn't. Albert and Rosebud were just friends. He wasn't a threat to their relationship. It's just that Rosebud was ready to settle down and Ronald wasn't. He is now though."

Cleo wondered if Taylor would take the hint about them. He didn't.

"Well, we may as well eat dinner. Have you eaten yet?" Cleo asked.

"No, I haven't."

"I put wine on ice. I'll pour you a glass while I finish the salmon."

"Are you sure you want me to stay?" he asked.

"You may as well, I've cooked now."

He took her chin in his hand. "You're not going to make it easy, are you?"

"Was I supposed to? It's your job. I understand you can't do anything about it. That doesn't mean I have to like it, does it?"

"No, it doesn't. And I understand the U.S. Attorney's position is different because I work with it every day. I read letters from distraught citizens and I talk to them daily."

"Which doesn't mean Judy should get leniency. You don't understand."

"More than you realize. I have to see the case from a wider view, not just from one perspective."

Cleo hoped because of their relationship he'd at least try to see it from her position. The fact that he didn't told her more than anything else that his feelings for her weren't as strong as hers for him.

"Apprehending Judy Gross would be a temporary fix. The people above her are still out there to continue this or indulge in some other form of fraud. If we can catch them, we can end this crime wave."

"I understand Taylor."

"No, you don't."

"We don't have to agree on it. I want them apprehended along with Judy."

"It's in the U.S. Attorney's office now. All the negotiations are done by them."

"They aren't doing a good job of it, are they?"

"You can always file a civil suit."

"You mean stand in line. They stole every dime they have. A lot of people are going to be suing."

Silence stretched again.

"Salmon's my favorite."

"I thought we'd celebrate with it." She turned and left the room.

She reappeared with his wine and they sat by the fire with stilted conversation until dinner was ready.

Though Taylor had expected some fallout from this, this was not how he had envisioned the evening.

Chapter 18

The next day, Ronald called again, inviting himself over to Cleo's for dinner and offering that he *would* invite them to Rosebud's, but she didn't have time to spend in the kitchen. They'd be over around nine.

Cleo wasn't in the mood for company, but it would give Taylor an opportunity to meet Ronald.

Ronald's gruff persona would be off-putting for most people, but Rosebud loved him, and Cleo could accept him. The most difficult endeavor would be to keep him from running her life.

Cleo fixed the old standby—steak and potatoes with salad for dinner. Ronald was a meat and potatoes man.

Ronald and Rosebud arrived first. Wearing a smidgen of makeup and black dress slacks with a flattering orange sweater, Rosebud looked more carefree than she had in months.

"Don't you look nice?" Cleo told her. "What can I get you to drink?"

"Got a beer?" Ronald asked.

Since Taylor liked Budweiser, she'd stocked up on that brand. "Budweiser okay?"

He nodded.

"I'll take wine," Rosebud said.

"I lit a fire. Go on in the family room. I'll get your drinks and join you."

Before she joined them, Taylor arrived wearing jeans and a blue shirt. Cleo made introductions.

Ronald and he immediately sized each other up as they shook hands.

Rosebud had called Cleo around ten that morning to find out what happened and Cleo gave her the abridged version trying not to let her discontent show.

Taylor was surprised when she called him today to invite him to meet Ronald at dinner. Now, Taylor glanced at her to gage her reaction. She offered him a saccharine smile.

He breathed deeply, knowing a battle was in order before it all was cleared up.

"Bud and I want to know what's going on with our little girl?"

"I am not a little girl. And it's all settled. We talked about it this morning, remember?" She handed Rosebud her wine and Ronald his beer. "I didn't invite you over to grill Taylor, just to meet him."

She raised an eyebrow at Taylor and asked, "Beer?"

"Sure," he nodded and sank comfortably in the wing chair.

Cleo disappeared into the kitchen again and put the steaks on the grill and returned with Taylor's beer.

"I want to hear what this here fellow has to say about the case," Ronald said.

Cleo started to interrupt again, but Taylor stopped it.

"Cleo isn't under suspicion. We've arrested three of the people involved and are about to make more arrests."

"Well of course she isn't under suspicion," Ronald declared, affronted. "This is our Cleo here," he professed as if that said it all.

"Do you know Ronnie," Rosebud cut in. "Taylor lives on a boat at the Marina. It's nice, too. Hattie and I had dinner there a while back."

He looked at Rosebud as if she were crazy. "That's nice, Bud. I'm taking care of business now, Puddin'." He patted her hand and turned back to Taylor.

Cleo expected Rosebud to erupt like a whaling banshee, but she merely shrugged her shoulders as if to say, "you two are on your own."

"Young man, I need to get this settled before we leave. Me and Bud here can't stay too long."

"I hope you can stay for dinner," Cleo said. "It's almost ready." She glared at Ronald. "There's nothing to settle."

Taylor stood. "I thought I heard something rattling under my hood on my way over. Why don't we go out, Ronald, while I check it out."

"This isn't the age where the men go off to take care of the 'little lady's' business while the woman patiently waits." Cleo scowled at both of them.

"I can take care of myself, Cleo." He kissed her on the nose.

Ronnie waited by the door.

"We'll be right back—as soon as I check under my hood," Taylor said.

He snatched Ronald's jacket out of the closet, handed it to him and donned his own.

Cleo and Rosebud watched them from the window.

"I can't believe their male posturing. Leave the little women in the house while they take care of men's business."

The said men were talking animatedly outside. They didn't even look at the car.

"Let them be. You know Ronnie doesn't have any children of his own. We're getting married and he likes playing Dad." She announced it as if it were an afterthought.

"Oh, Rosebud." She clutched the woman's arms. "It's final?"

"Yes. Christmas next year when he returns."

She hugged the older woman. "I'm so happy for you!"

"Says he misses me. Didn't understand how much he loved me until I wasn't there anymore."

Cleo smiled, happy for her friend.

"Let's check on those steaks," Rosebud said.

The steaks were done and Cleo put dinner on the table. "Tell the men the food is ready. I hope they've ironed everything out."

Cleo never discovered the particulars of their talk. Taylor would only say they talked.

She knew that much.

And still, she hadn't heard from Taylor, Cleo thought as she lifted another box in the storage room to one side and mopped and polished the floor. The muscles in her back and arms strained. She'd done the other side yesterday. Now both sides of the room were polished. The floors hadn't looked that good since she moved into the shop.

"Well done if I do say so myself."

Having completed the chore to her satisfaction, she entered her pristine office to go over last month's sales figures, using the opportunity to eat a sandwich at her desk. She cleaned the office two days ago with Rosebud hovering about trying to get her to stop. Hard work never hurt a soul.

But today she'd been able to do her work without Tina or Rosebud's intrusion, thank goodness.

After giving the floor ample time to dry, she returned to the storage room to arrange the boxes.

As she lifted the first box, she wondered for the fiftieth time why Taylor hadn't visited her this week—at her house or her shop. Didn't she tell him she didn't blame him for the outcome of the investigation? What more could she do? Of course she'd been disappointed. Who wouldn't be?

Perhaps the relationship was a passing thing. Now that the investigation was over, so were they.

Cleo plopped in a chair. How could it be after all they'd shared? He'd gone far beyond the call of duty. He didn't have to complete her bathroom, did he? And yet he did—for free. So why did he do it if he didn't at least care for her?

Thinking of Taylor, Cleo got up and lifted the next box.

In half an hour she had the storage room exactly the way she wanted it.

The bank deposit was made, her paperwork was done, her blends were mixed, the rooms were cleaned. If she worked hard enough, perhaps she'd sleep tonight instead of tossing and turning.

But what else was there to do? She could always straighten shelves in the store.

Cleo rushed to the store. Rosebud and Tina were hovering by the cash register talking. Well, wasn't it nice of them to have spare time when the display table Tina had set up was a mess?

Cleo marched over to it and started tidying it.

"Cleo?" Rosebud said.

"Yes?" she answered moving a tall painted bottle of bath beads near the sponge and looking back to inspect it.

"Could I talk to you in your office a moment, please?"

Cleo looked up. "Give me a few minutes to finish this, will you?"

"That can wait. I want to talk to you now."

Cleo looked at the older woman who was tapping her foot impatiently. What was it now? Cleo wondered. "All right, Rosebud. But make it quick. I want to get this done." She marched ahead of Rosebud.

The older woman closed the door behind her.

Cleo plopped in the seat behind her desk.

"You've got to let this thing with Judy go."

"She's been arrested. There's nothing I can do about it now. I've let it go."

"But have you really let it go?" Rosebud asked skeptically. "Maybe you need to think about it."

"What makes you think I haven't?"

"You're working like a madwoman. You're driving everybody here crazy with your cleaning and your nit-picking."

"What's wrong with having a clean shop?"

Rosebud threw up her hands. "You can eat Sunday breakfast off the storage room floor for goodness sake, child. Talk to Taylor and settle whatever dispute you have so the rest of us can have some peace. It'll settle your nerves, too."

"We don't have a dispute, Rosebud. I guess that now that the investigation—at least my end of it—is over, he's found other things to do." Cleo tapped impatiently on the desk.

"That man loves you."

Her fingers stilled. "Then why hasn't he called. Why hasn't he come to the store or my house. A week ago, a day didn't pass when I didn't see him. I haven't seen him one day this week. You tell me if those are the actions of a man in love."

"You've run him away, is what you've done. And now

you're running around here like a crazy woman. You've probably cleaned your whole doggone house by now."

Cleo looked away sheepishly.

"I haven't run him away," she finally said.

"You blame him for the actions the U.S. Attorney has taken."

"Taylor is the investigator, not the U.S. Attorney. I don't hold him responsible for that and he knows it. I told him so. What more can I do?"

"If I don't believe you. You know he doesn't."

"And what can I do about that!"

"Let me tell you something. You love that man. You hear me? And he loves you. Don't you mope around here cleaning yourself half to death. You've lost weight and you look more like a dishrag than the beautiful young woman you are."

"Well, thank you very much for your concern."

Rosebud ignored her snappish tone. "You've got some choices to make gal. No need to use that sass with me. You're like a daughter to me."

"Rosebud you always use that line when you want to get your way."

"It's true and you know it. I wouldn't lead you wrong."

Cleo blew out a breath. "I know that."

"He's done his job. It's out of his hands. Now let it go."

"Rosebud . . ."

"He investigated, he found evidence, and he turned it in. There's nothing else he can do. And you had better get over it."

"I am, Rosebud. You're not telling me anything I don't know. I told you I know he's done his best."

"There are very few good men out here with sound jobs. You better grab him while you can."

"I thought you had those bad vibes about him."

"The bad vibes were because he was a spy. I was right about that. But I know a good man when I see him."

"I can't put in his heart what isn't there." Her voice cracked.

Rosebud softened. "He loves you. He's not out there playing games. You let him go, you'll regret it for the rest of your life."

"Rosebud . . ."

"Now go home. We'll take care of the store. Take some time to think instead of running away from it by cleaning."

"There are too many memories there."

"Go home, Cleo. And think about it. I can't tell you what to do. You've got to come up with the solution that's best for you. There's nothing else to do here. You've cleaned everything."

"I'll leave when I finish that table."

"Give the rest of us something to do, will you? We work here, too, you know."

"All right. If I'm not needed here, I will go."

Cleo snatched up her coat and left.

She loved Rosebud, but the woman didn't know what she was talking about. If Taylor loved her, he wouldn't have spent the week away from her. He would call, he would visit. And he would have been willing to make a commitment.

Cleo walked into her sparkling-clean house. Since she couldn't sleep at night, she'd used the time to clean. It was seven-thirty.

Lighting the fire or candles would only remind her

of Taylor, so she pulled a salad out the refrigerator and nibbled on it at the kitchen table. Most of it she threw away.

She got in the Jacuzzi to soak her sore muscles, but that reminded her of Taylor, too.

Would her house ever be hers again?

At nine, Cleo went to bed, hoping for a decent night's sleep. But she only tossed and turned thinking of Taylor.

She didn't blame him for the outcome of the investigation. She told him that. There was no reason for him not to believe her.

She knew how hard he'd worked on the case. How hard he'd worked at her house and her store.

And she understood his part ended with the investigation.

God, she loved that man. Cleo punched the pillow. She couldn't make him love her in return.

They were so good together. She replayed the night they'd laid on the couch spoon fashion. He was so comfortable to be with. To talk to. They didn't have to do anything special to enjoy each other. Just being together was all it took.

She also replayed the next night when she told him she didn't hold him responsible.

He doesn't believe me, she thought. And then Cleo thought, *I wouldn't believe me either.* She'd been standoffish and cold afterward even though, intellectually, she didn't hold him responsible, in her heart she did because she didn't like the way it all ended.

He'd seen what was in her heart.

"I've got to talk to him."

Cleo jumped out of bed, and ran to the closet and

grabbed her coat, snatched her keys off the dresser, stepped into her shoes, and went to see Taylor.

She needed to talk to him tonight.

Cleo used the key Taylor had given her for the security gate to enter the marina and raced down the pier, against the blowing wind. Suddenly she realized she'd worn three-inch heels. "I'm going to either drown in that freezing water or break my neck," she mumbled to herself.

She finally made it to Taylor's boat and remembered it wasn't a house and wouldn't have a doorbell. Was he going to hear her knock?

She pounded on the fiberglass siding. He didn't answer. She'd seen a light as she'd walked up, so he must be awake. She pounded some more. She didn't holler for fear of waking the people on boats nearby.

She shivered as the wind whipping under the coat reached her backside.

She'd forgotten to put on street clothes. Then she remembered she didn't comb her hair. She must look a fright. Quickly, she finger-combed her hair.

She heard footsteps behind her. It was the middle of the night. Out in the open wasn't the safest place for a woman to be. She forgot about waking anybody and screamed, "Taylor!" and banged rapidly on the side.

"I'm here," a voice behind her answered.

Cleo whipped around tethering. He ran up to support her.

"Why are you on a deck in high-heel shoes? Are you trying to kill yourself?" he shouted, holding on to her as he helped her walk.

"Of course not. Like a fool, I came to see you." He was supposed to be happy to see her not snapping at her. Holding onto him for dear life, Cleo bent to take off the shoes, the freezing deck shocking her bare feet. Taylor held the flap for her to step aboard the deck, and he hurriedly opened the cabin door.

She sank her toes into the blessed warm carpet.

"I'll take your coat," Taylor said.

Cleo wavered a moment then unbuttoned it and handed it to him.

"Are you wearing that nightgown for the usual reason?" he asked with a slight grin.

"I was in bed when I decided to come over. I kind of forgot about . . ." She ran a business with several employees. How was she to tell him she forgot to put on her clothes when she decided to come over?

"Come on and sit down while I fix something to warm you up," he offered.

"I could use something," she said. Cleo didn't sit though. She followed him to the galley and watched as he started the Mrs. Tea.

"You've purchased a new appliance since I saw you last."

"When I'm in love with a tea lover, what else could I do?"

"Taylor . . ."

"Yes, you heard me. I love you."

Not expecting that declaration, she choked and Taylor pounded her on the back.

She put her hands to his face, her mouth working and nothing coming out. She coughed once more.

"Taylor," her eyes misted. "I love you."

"Then you'll marry me? I don't have a ring yet . . . ."

Cleo squealed and leaped on him as she smothered his face with kisses. "I don't care about a ring," she whispered between kisses.

Taylor squeezed her, getting in a few kisses of his own.

"I thought you only wanted an affair."

"Why?" he asked baffled.

"Because you'd never commit, that's why."

"An endless affair never occurred to me. I just wanted the business of this investigation behind me before I asked. I didn't want it hanging over us."

"I like your boat, but I'm not living on it."

"I won't ask you to. Only that you hire more workers and spend more time on it with me."

Cleo stilled. "You know if my customers get nervous about what has occurred, I could lose my business."

"And I'll still love you and marry you."

"I don't hold you responsible for what the U.S. Attorney has done. I was hurt . . . ."

He put a finger to her lips to silence her. "I know. It was a shock and you needed time to get over it. Trust is the very essence of love."

"I'm glad you understand. But do you understand how much I appreciate all that you've done for me?" She whispered.

He tightened his arms around her. "Yes, I do."

"Taylor I'll marry you, but I want to wait until after this case is over."

"I want to be with you through the ordeal," he whispered. "When spring comes, we're spending weekends on this yacht as husband and wife."

"Husband and wife. That has a nice ring to it."

Epilogue

"Cast off, Taylor," Cleo called from the helm.

"You're a bossy one, aren't you?"

Winded, Taylor joined her in the helm, taking the coffee Cleo handed to him.

"Aye, aye, Captain. Let's go."

Cleo eased the *Serenity* out the slip, enjoying the view every bit as much as she did the first time when Taylor had steered.

Sitting in the captain's chair, she put a hand protectively on her abdomen and smiled. Her womb was just beginning to round with their first baby.

The trial was long over and had guaranteed national publicity—thanks to the U.S. Attorney office's need to get out the word on mail fraud. The postal service was proud that they'd broken a case of this size and that this case, among so many inconclusive mail-fraud investigations was resolved.

More than fifty people were involved, including Albert who was caught at Dulles Airport.

Soon after the arrests, Cleo had made her circuit on *60 Minutes, Nightline, Good Morning America* and dozens of other shows. Her business quadrupled overnight.

The only temporary blemish was that, now that Cleo was pregnant, she couldn't use the hot Jacuzzi she loved so much. Doctor's orders.

She glanced at Taylor. They spent half their time on the *Serenity*.

Taylor had mentioned getting a bigger house, but Cleo wasn't ready to move.

Happily married to Ronald, Rosebud was now the shop's manager. And she'd had to hire a full-time staff for mail order.

Everyone was ecstatic about the baby. Rosebud and Cleo's mom already had plans mapped out for their first grandchild.

ABOUT THE AUTHOR

Bestselling author Candice Poarch's sister first intro-
duced her to romances and it wasn't long before she
craved to write romances of her own featuring African-
American heroes and heroines. Candice is a member
of several writers groups. She lives in Springfield, Virginia with her family.

Dear Readers:

Thank you for so many kind letters.

I hope you enjoyed your time with Cleo and Taylor. As much as I enjoyed writing about them, my next book will revisit Nottoway, Virginia for Jonathan's story. I've received many requests for him. Gladys Jones will be in seventh heaven when Jonathan falls in love with her daughter, Johanna who returns to her home town to transform the only ramshackle hotel into a distinguished historical beauty. She's nothing like her mother!

Again, thank you for your support. Please visit my web page at www.erols.com/cpoarch.

I love hearing from readers. You may reach me at:

Candice Poarch
P.O. Box 291
Springfield, VA 22150

AND FOR THE HOLIDAYS . . .
COMING IN DECEMBER . . .

FOOLISH HEART   (0-7860-0593-9, $4.99/$6.50)
by Felicia Mason
CEO Coleman Heart III inherited his family's chain of department stores
and focused only on saving it from bankruptcy. Business consultant Sonja
Pride became the only person he felt he could trust. But Sonja had a debt
to pay the Heart family, and being close to Coleman seemed the perfect
way to make them pay. Until she found out he was a caring, honorable
man to whom she could give away her heart.

DARK INTERLUDE   (0-7860-0594-7, $4.99/$6.50)
by Dianne Mayhew
Sissi Adams and Percy Duvall had a relationship based on trust. But when
Sissi admitted that she didn't want children, Percy was devastated. And
when they discovered that Sissi was pregnant and that she miscarried,
Percy broke off the relationship believing she aborted their child. Years
later, Sissi is unhappily engaged to another, unable to forget her true love.
She places Percy on the guest list of a celebration for her upcoming
wedding for one last chance to see if they were made for each other.

SECRETS   (0-7860-0595-5, $4.99/$6.50)
by Marilyn Tyner
Samantha Desmond raised her young stepsister, Jessica. To keep Jessica
from calculating relatives, Samantha pretends Jessica is her daughter and
relocates. When she meets pediatrician Alex Mackenzie, she fights the
attraction between them to keep him from getting too close. But Alex
finds out the truth about Jessica and his trust in Samantha is broken. They
soon learn that neither can do without each other and their love.

OUT OF THE BLUE   (0-7860-0596-3, $4.99/$6.50)
by Janice Sims
On a research trip to frigid Russian waters in pursuit of the blue whale,
marine biologist Gaea Maxwell doesn't expect to meet corporate attorney
Micah Cavanaugh—a man capable of thawing her frozen heart. Micah
was asked to recruit Gaea for a teaching position at a private college. He
didn't expect her to be a beautiful, charming woman. She refuses the
position and returns home to Key West, Florida. Micah is more than
disappointed. He follows her to Florida, determined to show that his love
runs as deep as the ocean.

Available wherever paperbacks are sold, or order direct from the Pub-
lisher. Send cover price plus 50¢ per copy for mailing and handling to
Kensington Publishing Corp., Consumer Orders, or call (toll free) 888-
345-BOOK, to place your order using Mastercard or Visa. Residents of
New York and Tennessee must include sales tax. DO NOT SEND CASH.

AND FOR THE HOLIDAYS ...

SEASON'S GREETINGS   (0-7860-0601-3, $4.99/$6.50)
by Margie Walker, Roberta Gayle and Courtni Wright
Margie Walker provides hope to a scrooge in form of a woman in her moving Christmas tale. When Hope Ellison and her young son melt Stone Henderson's frozen heart, he will do anything to keep them ... including go up against her ex-love. In Roberta Gayle's perky Kwanzaa celebration, Geri Tambray-Smith looks for a date before matchmaking uncles interfere. Luckily, Professor Wilton Greer is a willing accomplice in it for research purposes, who finally learns what love is all about. Courtni Wright rings in the New Year with a new love for Pat Bowles, who is looking to get away on a New Year's Caribbean cruise and finds love with a seductive stranger.

CHANCES ARE   (0-7860-0602-1, $4.99/$6.50)
by Donna Hill
Dione Williams, founder of a home for teenage mothers and their babies, and television producer, Garrett Lawrence, were drawn to each other from the start. Only she was a young mother herself and Garrett's cynical view of "irresponsible" teen mothers puts them at extreme odds. But 'tis the season of hope and a chance at new beginnings.

LOVE'S CELEBRATION   (0-7860-0603-X, $4.99/$6.50)
by Monica Jackson
Two years have past since Teddi Henderson's husband picked up and left her and her daughter behind with no explanation. She had returned to her hometown in Kansas to start anew, but the Kwanzaa celebration always brought memories of J.T. This time it has brought him back in person ... with dangerous secrets—he is a government agent. Can Teddi put her faith in him again and start anew with the man she has always loved?

A RESOLUTION OF LOVE   (0-7860-0604-8, $4.99/$6.50)
by Jacquelin Thomas
Daryl Larsen's biological clock was telling her it was time to settle down and have children. This New Year's she's determined to find Mr. Right, and she is sure she sees him in pro basketball player Sheldon Turner. Even though he has a reputation as a ladies man, and he sees nothing amiss with a life of beautiful women and momentary passion. Sheldon soon begins to feel something special for Daryl, whose persistent caring and honesty has him seeing life differently.

Available wherever paperbacks are sold, or order direct from the Publisher. Send cover price plus 50¢ per copy for mailing and handling to Kensington Publishing Corp., Consumer Orders, or call (toll free) 888-345-BOOK, to place your order using Mastercard or Visa. Residents of New York and Tennessee must include sales tax. DO NOT SEND CASH.

ALL FOR LOVE   (0-7860-0309-X, $4.99)
by Raynetta Manees

ONLY HERS   (0-7860-0255-7, $4.99)
by Francis Ray

HOME SWEET HOME   (0-7860-0276-X, $4.99)
by Rochelle Alers

Available wherever paperbacks are sold, or order direct from the Publisher. Send cover price plus 50¢ per copy for mailing and handling to Kensington Publishing Corp., Consumer Orders, or call (toll free) 888-345-BOOK, to place your order using Mastercard or Visa. Residents of New York and Tennessee must include sales tax. DO NOT SEND CASH.